Tuck Me In, Mummy

Look for these SpineChillers™ Mysteries

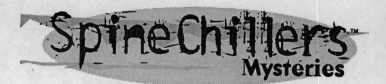

Tuck Me In, Mummy

Fred E. Katz

Thomas Nelson, Inc.
Nashville

Published in Nashville, Tennessee, by Tommy Nelson™, a division of Thomas Nelson, Inc., SpineChillers™ Mysteries is a trademark of Thomas Nelson, Inc.

Scripture quoted from the *International Children's Bible, New Century Version,* copyright © 1983, 1986, 1988 by Word Publishing, Dallas, Texas. Used by permission.

Storyline: Tim Ayers

Library of Congress Cataloging-in-Publication Data
Katz, Fred E.
   Tuck me in, mummy / Fred E. Katz.
      p. cm. — (SpineChillers Mysteries; 9)
   Summary: While preparing to spend the night in a museum exhibition of the treasures of King Tut, twelve-year-old Jessica and her friends become obsessed with mummies and stumble upon several strange incidents.
   ISBN 0-8499-4052-4
   [1. Mummies—Fiction. 2. Museums—Fiction. 3. Tutankhamen, King of Egypt—Fiction. 4. Egypt—Civilization—To 332 B. C.—Fiction 5. Christian Life—Fiction. 6. Mystery and detective stories.]
I. Title. II. Series: Katz, Fred E. SpineChillers mysteries: 9.
PZ7.K1573Tu 1997
[Fic]—dc21   97–11095
                                                      CIP
                                                      AC

Printed in the United States of America.

97 98 99 00 01 02 QKP 9 8 7 6 5 4 3 2 1

It was the mummy's hand. Kevin had tripped on the mummy's hand which stretched across the doorway into the treasure vault of the pyramid. He scrambled out of the dusty, smelly tomb and raced down the passage to the next opening. It led back into the treasure room. He yelled, "John, Andrew, Rudy, where are you?" No answer came back. All he heard were the moans of the mummy behind him.

The treasure room glittered with gold and jewels. The mummy had enough wealth to buy what he needed when he went into the spirit world. Unfortunately for Kevin and his friends, this mummy had stayed behind to protect his fortune.

Kevin saw a ray of light breaking through a crack in the wall. "John, are you there? Andrew, where are you? Rudy, help!" he yelled. The mummy staggered into the treasure vault and took a long, teetering step toward Kevin. The boy backed closer to the wall. He wished he were small enough to fit through the crack, but not even a super-crash diet would help him now.

The mummy stepped closer and Kevin gulped. He looked around at the goblets, jewelry, and rope made out of gold. For a moment his eyes sparkled. He had an idea. He grabbed the rope and twisted the end into a lasso. Near the wall sat a statue of a bird. It was more than twenty feet tall.

Kevin swung the lasso at the big bird as the mummy took another step closer. The golden loop bounced off the bird's beak and came crashing back to the floor. The mummy would be on him in another three steps. Kevin reeled in the rope and tossed it again. The mummy took another step.

The loop dropped over the bird's long, sculptured beak. Kevin yanked and the rope went snug. Just in time! The mummy's next step would be right on top of him. Kevin grabbed the golden rope tightly and leaped into the air. The mummy's hands came so close to grabbing him that he could feel the breeze of their movement as he swung by.

The golden rope carried him to the far side of the room as the mummy stood and stared at his hands in disbelief. *I've got to get out of here, but I need to find my friends first*, Kevin thought. He yelled for them again, but there was still no answer.

The mummy staggered to his right and took a shaky step toward the boy. Kevin's eyes darted around the room. There was very little space to maneuver away from the mummy. He yelled again for his friends. "Where did they go?" he thought aloud.

His attention was jolted by the mummy's growling voice: "Swift death to all who enter. Swift death to all who enter."

Kevin backed closer to the wall and started sliding along it toward an opening. As the mummy got closer, the boy grabbed a clay bowl and tossed it. It smashed against the mummy and crumbled to the floor. The beast screamed with a voice that had been silent for centuries, "Swift death to all who enter!"

"I don't think so," Kevin said. He leaped on top of the mountain of gold and jewels. He scrambled over it and dropped against the cracked wall. He pounded on it and yelled again for his friends. "Hey, I need some help in here. Where are you guys?"

The boy turned and saw the gift-wrapped ghoul reaching for him. He stared into the blackness of the slits over the mummy's eyes. He had no place to go. Kevin closed his eyes and heard once more, "Swift death to all who enter." The boy waited for the swift death that the mummy promised.

He felt hands grip him, but they weren't from the front, they were from behind. He didn't feel two hands; he felt six. They yanked backward, and he tumbled into several inches of dust.

Kevin was afraid to look up, but then he heard Rudy's voice say, "That ought to teach you for getting lost."

"What happened?" he asked.

John was the first to answer. "We could hear you but couldn't find a way to get to you. Until we discovered the crack in the wall. It had to be a secret door. Andrew finally found the secret latch."

As Kevin stood up he asked, "What happened to the mummy?"

"The door closed too fast for him to make it. Too bad, huh." Rudy said.

Andrew reached down and pulled Kevin to his feet. "We better get out of here," he told the others.

The four went slowly through the dark, musty corridor. The only light came from Rudy's small flashlight. No one talked, but fear and tension were written on their faces. After several minutes Andrew whispered, "What's that? I think I see light around that corner." He ran ahead of the others and slid on the dirty floor, coming to a dead stop at a rock that blocked the passage out of the pyramid.

The other three pulled up behind him. John asked, "How are we going to move this rock?"

Rudy grabbed a long pole that was nearly covered in the floor's dust. "I think this will push it out of the way." She lodged it under the rock and the four heaved against the rock. It moved! They squeezed out of the passage and into the bright Egyptian sun. In seconds, eight feet were kicking up dust as they raced to the archeologists' camp. There they dived into John's tent. His father, the head of the archeologists, sat in his chair poring over his notes from the day. They had found a number of interesting items, and now he needed to catalog them. He raised his head, bothered by the intrusion, and said, "What is going on? I'm trying to work here. Why aren't the four of you at the pyramid for the dig?"

John spoke up, "Dad, we were at the pyramid. Rudy found a shaft and we followed it. It took us into the treasure room and then to the king's resting place."

Kevin butted in, "Only the mummy wasn't resting. The moment we picked up a piece of the treasure, the outer coffin slid open. Then the inner coffin top flew back and out crawled the mummy."

"Hold it, kids," John's dad said. "Are you trying to tell me that we've been digging for weeks and you four have accidentally discovered the treasure room and the king's coffins?"

"Dad, we found it. And the mummy is alive and walking around," John excitedly told his father.

"You know, sometimes when we get deep inside one of those centuries-old pyramids, the lighting and dust can make you think that you're seeing things that aren't there," John's dad said with doubt in his voice.

Andrew grabbed the other three kids and pulled them out of the tent. He said, "Come on. I don't think we're going to get anyone to believe us around here. We'll have to come up with a way to put that mummy back in his coffin ourselves."

The four walked into the heart of the camp and sat at the table and benches used for eating. Rudy asked, "Any suggestions? If John's dad doesn't believe us, I don't think that we'll get anyone else to either."

The kids sat silently looking at each other until Kevin said, "We've got to find some way to cover any entrances that are open."

"Right. If all the passages are blocked, then the mummy can't get out," Rudy added. "But we need to do it when no one is watching. If someone sees us, those passages will get opened up again right away. We'll have to go tonight after dark."

"After dark?" exclaimed Andrew.

"Yep," Rudy said. "It's the only way. We'll meet back here at midnight."

The rest of the evening dragged by. The friends retired to their tents and crawled into their sleeping bags fully dressed. They didn't want to wake anyone when they sneaked out later. As midnight came, Rudy slipped out and went to the table and benches. Soon John and Andrew met her. They waited for Kevin. The minutes ticked by very slowly.

"That guy would be late for his own funeral," John said.

Rudy gulped and added, "Don't say that. We could all be early for our own funerals if this doesn't work out. Let's go wake him up and get going."

They walked toward his tent. Once there, John noticed that the sand was scuffed, like a battle had occurred. Rudy pointed out a string of footprints heading off toward the pyramid. As they looked in that direction, they saw Kevin being dragged away by the mummy.

3

"Is that what I think it is?" Rudy gulped as she spoke.

The two boys stood stunned, nodding their heads. John finally spoke, "How could that have happened? I thought the mummy would stay in the pyramid. How did it get out?"

"We didn't put the rock back," Andrew answered. "It got out just like we did. But why is it after Kevin? It's so dead-set—I didn't mean to use that word, sorry."

"I don't think we've got time to figure that one out. We've got to get to the pyramid and save Kevin," Rudy said as she leaped into the first step of a high speed run. John and Andrew were only seconds behind her. By the time they went over the sand dune, they could see the shadowy figure of the mummy pulling a fighting, kicking Kevin into the hole at the side of the pyramid.

When they got to the opening, the mummy had already covered it with the rock. "It took all four of us to move it before. What now?" Andrew asked with panic in his voice.

8

Rudy answered solemnly, "We go around to the front and go through the treasure room again."

"But that's where the mummy will be. We won't be able to sneak up on him," Andrew complained.

John said with resignation, "Do we have any choice?"

The three ran to the side of the pyramid where the workers had been digging. One of the Egyptians was supposed to be guarding the entrance, but he had already begun to snore. Carefully and quietly they slipped by. The musty air inside the pyramid made Andrew's nose tickle. He could feel a sneeze coming on, and his sneezes registered on the Richter scale. Rudy saw it coming. She pivoted on her heels and shot her arm toward Andrew's face. Her finger slid up under his nose and stopped the sneeze just in time. She grabbed him and pulled him deeper into the pyramid.

"That was close, real close," Andrew said with relief, but he spoke too soon. They were only thirty feet into the passage when the tickle in Andrew's nostrils became more than he could bear. Without warning, he sneezed. The echo sounded like an explosion. The stone walls felt like they shook, and dust dropped from their cracks.

John and Rudy looked at him with anger. "There goes our hope of sneaking up on the mummy, Andrew."

"Yeah, nice going," John added.

"Sorry, but you know I'm allergic to dust," he said apologetically. "All we can do now is hurry and grab Kevin before he gets eaten or something." They picked up their pace and walked as fast as they could behind Rudy's dim flashlight. When they came to the secret entrance to the treasure room, the two boys lifted Rudy up to grab the small, carved bird statue. She pulled down on it and the panel began to slide open. John pulled something from his pocket.

"What are you doing?" Rudy asked.

"I'm always losing my house keys, so Dad got me one of those things that beeps when you clap. I think it can help us here. When we're ready to leave, all we have to do is clap and follow the sound back," he told them.

"I hope it works," Andrew said. The three kids started into the treasure room. They didn't need the flashlight any longer; the room was lit by four torches, one at each corner of the room. Andrew stopped suddenly, and Rudy and John bumped into him from behind.

They stood staring at Kevin. He was dressed in a ceremonial Egyptian sun god outfit and was tied to a golden altar. They didn't see the mummy anywhere, but they knew he couldn't be far away. Cautiously, Andrew approached his friend Kevin, who was gagged. His eyes said everything that he needed to say. He was scared. The mummy planned to sacrifice him to Ra, the sun god.

The three kids tried to untie the ropes binding their friend. "They're too tight," John said. Before he could say another word, Rudy dug a gold ceremonial dagger from the piles of treasure. She slipped it under the ropes and started cutting. As she got to the last one, the kids heard a loud growling voice. "Swift death to all who enter. Ra angry. Wants sacrifice."

Andrew grabbed a large goblet and tossed it at the mummy, saying, "That's for using such poor grammar." The mummy staggered and then stood erect again. John scooped up a bowl and pitched a winning touchdown pass at the mummy's head. It staggered again.

Rudy finished cutting Kevin free and pulled him from the altar. He yelled at the others, "We've got to get out of here. This isn't the only mummy here. He's got relatives and servants, and they're all walking around. Even the mummy's mommy is here." As if on cue, a second mummy staggered into the room. Together the two moved slowly in the direction of the four kids.

The kids backed into a wall covered with an intricately woven tapestry. Trapped!

"What now?" Rudy asked.

Suddenly, two gauze-wrapped hands reached from behind the tapestry and grabbed her.

4

"Swift death to all who enter," growled a voice right behind my head. I leaped three feet off the couch and twisted around quickly in mid-air. "Benjamin, stop it! You know that part of the video scares me," I yelled as I picked up the remote control and stopped the movie. "I'm sorry my brother ruined the film."

"That's all right," Becca said. "I don't think I should be watching stuff like this a few days before we spend a night in an Egyptian pyramid."

"A simulated pyramid," Adam said. "Remember, they only brought the inside stuff from Egypt. We're not going to Egypt. If there's a mummy roaming around in a pyramid, it won't be anywhere near us."

"Besides, *The Curse of the Tomb Raiders* is only a movie. How can you be scared of a movie?" Benjamin asked.

I often get frustrated with my twin brother, Benjamin. It's kind of strange having only one other sibling and having that one be your twin. I'm just glad that we aren't identical twins. Sharing the same birth-day, classrooms, and teachers is enough for me.

I am Jessica Hoffman, the first and only. Benjamin and I are the only twins at our middle school. We're alike in a lot of ways except for our taste in books. Benjamin likes horror and ghost stories. Somehow he enjoys being scared. Me, I like mysteries. They have an element of excitement, and I love to figure out who did it. It makes my brain work overtime.

Our father, Dr. James K. Hoffman, is well known as an Egyptologist to museum- and history-type people, but not to kids my age. A lot of college students use his books for their classes on ancient Egyptian history. He's an authority on the subject, I guess. He also teaches the history of the Bible. We hear so many stories about Bible characters in our house that we often compare events in our life to them. Dad's books on Bible history are almost best-sellers. He's a professor at Keaton College, only a few miles from our house. It's just around the block from our school, Keaton Christian Middle School.

Mom works in the bookstore at the college. She really loves books, so it's the perfect place for her to work while she finishes up her degree at Keaton. It's kind of funny that Dad teaches at the college Mom attends.

But that's enough about the family. Benjamin and I had invited Adam and Becca over to watch a movie with us. They're our best friends. We go to middle school together and attend the same church. This is a great year for us because we're finally old enough to be part of the youth group at church. It's great to grow closer as friends and closer to God at the same time.

We rented the movie to get us all in the mood for our unusual camp-out, or rather camp-in.

Dad had promised us a camping trip. We'd made our plans and bought all the stuff. Then the Shield Museum called Dad. The museum was bringing the King Tutankhamen exhibit to town. Old King Tut himself, or at least his mummy, would be on display at the big museum downtown. They planned to construct a replica of his tomb's inner chambers. It would hold all the treasure, a stone casket called a sarcophagus, little *ushabti* statues believed to be servants for the afterlife, and hundreds more pieces.

The museum wanted to open on Saturday morning to the public, but it had one small snag. Only Dad knew how the different statues and jewelry should be placed. Yep, the only person who knew in the great big town of New Daley City was my dad. The museum asked him to help out the Friday night before the exhibit opened—the same night we had planned for our camping trip.

I don't know how Dad arranged it, but I think the

museum must've been desperate for his help. They agreed to let us kids spend the night in the replica of the pyramid. Dad thought it would be a once-in-a-lifetime opportunity for us to have a private viewing of the collection. He thought we'd really get a charge out of it. He was right.

Dad also got permission to translate the hieroglyphics on the inner caskets of some of the museum's Egyptian collection. These hieroglyphics were like early forms of the Egyptian Book of the Dead. He's wanted to work with that stuff for a long time.

So that's why we rented the mummy movie. I only wish Benjamin didn't like scary stories—and scaring others—so much. "Benjamin," I said, "I do hope you don't play jokes like that while we are in the museum. None of us would like it."

"I don't think I'll have to try to scare you. Being in that weird place with all the mummies will be scary enough," he answered.

Adam broke in, "It's supposed to be pretty creepy. I heard that one morning, when the security guard opened the place up, he found a mummy's hand. It was holding tight to the crash bar on the inside of the door. But the body wasn't there. The arm had been ripped off.

"The guard saw some sort of trail. It led all the way into the room where the museum keeps their mummies," he added. "Only I can't remember who told me that story."

Benjamin remarked, "Probably heard it on the news or something."

"No, I don't think so. It was a person who told me. Let me think," he scrunched up his eyebrows as if he were concentrating. "I remember now, it was . . ." Andrew stopped midsentence as a cloth-wrapped hand slid over his shoulder and fell at his feet.

Becca and I screamed. Then I looked at my brother and yelled, "Benjamin!"

Andrew looked up smiling, as he shifted his gaze from the hand at his feet to us, "Yeah, it was Benjamin who told that crazy story."

I stooped down and grabbed the hand. It was a rubber one that our grandfather had given Benjamin. Grandpa was a story all by himself. He used to travel with carnival sideshows. He made the third leg for the "Three-Legged Man" and extra arms for "Spider Man." The most interesting sideshow exhibit he worked on was the "Bodyless Wonder." That was Grandma. Grandpa made it look like she only had a head. He did it by arranging mirrors inside of a box she sat in. I don't tell many people about that. People look at you funny when you admit you're the grand-daughter of the "Bodyless Wonder."

Benjamin had wrapped the rubber hand up in thin strips of gauze. "That's it, brother dear," I said as I grabbed the hand. "I'm keeping this as physical evidence. I will present it to Mom and Dad tonight. Then, I'll sit back and enjoy watching your punishment."

"Come on, Jessica. I promise to stop. Just give me back my hand."

"Nope. Well, okay, I won't tell Mom and Dad, but I will keep this. You never know when you'll need an extra hand," I joked. I set the hand down on the coffee table out of Benjamin's reach.

Adam and Becca headed home, and Benjamin and I went to our rooms to finish our homework. I didn't say anything to Mom or Dad. But I think Benjamin held his breath all evening.

The next day, school went fast until I got to geography. Adam, Becca, Benjamin, and I had that class together. Becca has been my best friend since she moved in down the street from us. Adam and Benjamin have been friends since the playpen. The two of them were inseparable. I was glad—that way they didn't bother Becca and me.

Our geography teacher, Mrs. Tom, was very excited about our upcoming sleepover in the Shield Museum. She wanted us to give a report to the whole class on our time in the pyramid.

Mrs. Tom asked us to start by telling the others what we expected to find inside King Tut's tomb. I stood behind the other three in front of the class. I hoped that if I was in the back, I wouldn't have to do any of the talking. Benjamin is a lot better at that than I am.

Mrs. Tom looked at us and said, "Becca, you haven't grown up hearing everything in the world about Egypt like Jessica and Benjamin have. Tell us what you hope to learn in your time at the museum."

"This is going to be one of the greatest experiences of my life," she answered. "I want to see all the neat jewelry and stuff. Maybe they'll even let me bring a sample or two home with me." Becca laughed. "Seriously, though, I don't know much about ancient Egypt, and I'm hoping that I'll experience something really cool."

Mrs. Tom smiled and asked Adam, "What are you excited about?"

"The first thing I want to see is Tut's mummy. I hope to learn what kept him from rotting away like raw meat sitting in the sun," he said.

Mrs. Tom's lips twitched as she tried not to laugh. Then she looked right at me. I knew my name would be next out of her mouth. Instead she said, "Let's see, Benjamin, tell us what you hope to learn." I sighed with relief.

"There's so much that I can't really think of just one thing. But I do hope to see a mummy get up and walk around. I heard that one of them actually did come to life one night. It walked to the front door and tried to get out. Somehow its hand got torn off."

A mummy's hand reached out and grabbed Benjamin's shoulder. The entire class screamed in unison as he jumped.

"Jessica! I am surprised at you," Mrs. Tom said, shocked. "I'd expect your brother to come up with a fake mummy's hand in front of the class, but not you."

"Mrs. Tom, I owed him that one," I protested.

Becca came to my defense. "She's right, Mrs. Tom. Last night we were watching *The Curse of the Tomb Raiders* because we'd been thinking about our camping trip, and Benjamin scared us to death with that fake hand."

"Come on, you guys, this is supposed to be a report on the report we're going to do, not a pick-on-Benjamin report," Adam said.

"Okay. I think the best thing we could do is get back to the report," Mrs. Tom instructed. "Besides, you may get King Tut upset, and who knows what he might do."

Benjamin and I laughed, but I noticed that Adam and Becca seemed a little tense. My brother and I were used to all the ancient things from Egypt. We

21

never knew what we might find in the house next. Dad could bring home replicas of anything from a hundred-year-old beetle to an amulet that was believed to protect the wearer from evil. Dad made it all really interesting while he taught us the truth behind each piece.

Mrs. Tom continued, "Jessica, maybe you should finish by telling us what you'll be doing in the Shield Museum."

"We'll get there on Friday night. My dad will probably walk us around and show us all the different exhibits and then give us a quick lesson in hieroglyphics. After that, we'll set up camp in the replica of King Tut's inner chambers. If a mummy doesn't come in and eat us for his midnight snack, we'll leave the next morning before the museum opens."

Mrs. Tom smiled and asked, "Do you have anything special you want to study or see while you're in the museum?"

"Actually, I'd like to solve the mystery of the curse of King Tut . . ."

The bell rang and school ended for the day. Adam, Becca, Benjamin, and I usually get a ride home from one of our parents. But when the weather turns nice, which isn't very often around our part of the country, we walk the few blocks. As I grabbed my books from my locker, one of the girls from geography class stopped me.

She said, "I was at the Shield Museum last week when they were installing the inner chambers. It looked really cool. I was wondering about the curse that you mentioned. Aren't you guys afraid of it? Isn't King Tut supposed to kill anyone who touches his stuff? What happens if he really shows up?"

"My dad is an Egyptologist," I answered. "If the curse were real or if he thought there was any danger, he wouldn't be taking us to the museum. While I'm there, I hope to find proof that the curse is only a hoax. But I also think that we'll have a great time. With my dad there arranging the exhibit, we might even get to hold some of the promotional pieces."

"Wow, that's cool," she said just before Benjamin showed up and grabbed me. She was right. It was going to be cool. As we walked in the sun toward our house, the other three talked about the test coming up in our advanced math class. But I was thinking about how blessed we were to have an opportunity to spend the night in the museum. God had given my family lots of blessings, and I wanted to remember to mark this trip down as one of them. We got to our house. The other three were behind me as I grabbed the front door handle.

Before I twisted it, Becca called me, "Jessica, give me a call later."

"Sure. I'll ask my dad if there's anything special that we'll need to add to our camping gear. See you later," I called back to her. I turned to go into the house. Benjamin was only a few steps behind me as I pushed the door open and took a step inside.

Something leaped out at me. Startled, I discovered I was staring into the blank eyes of a wrinkled-faced, gauze-wrapped mummy. I screamed, and Benjamin leaped backward about four feet into the front yard.

7

The mummy tumbled on top of me. I kicked and tossed my arms around while I screamed for Benjamin to help me. In my heart I was calling out to God: *Lord, in the Book of Psalms it says that you'll protect us from our enemies that are all around us. Father, this one is all over me. Please help me now.* God would be my only help in this situation. My twin brother was too busy racing away to safety to do me any good.

I couldn't get the mummy off me! Then, almost magically, it began to float in the air away from my body. I don't believe in mummies that have mystical powers, but this one was trying hard to change my mind. I swung my fist at it, but it was already out of my reach. I tried again, but it called, "Stop! Don't hurt the mummy."

"Dad?" I asked.

"Of course it's me. Who else would bring a model of a mummy into the house? Please don't destroy my favorite classroom visual aid," Dad answered as he laughed at me.

"Dad, it scared me. Why didn't you leave it in the car or something? Do we have to display a fake Egyptian mummy in our entryway?"

"It wouldn't be safe in the car. Besides it's nothing but a bona fide, genuine, copy of a well-preserved coupla-thousand-years-old man," he said as he leaned the mummy against the wall. He turned and grabbed my extended hand and pulled me to my feet.

"Thanks, Dad. That really scared me for a minute." I then tried to change the subject. "What time is supper? I've got a lot of homework, and I don't want to be up too late. A girl's got to get her sleep before she hangs out with a bunch of dead people in an ancient tomb," I told him.

"About five. Mom has her Red Cross safety and first-aid training this evening, so she won't be joining us for supper. And if your brother can get over his fear and come inside, he can join us for a nice meal later on," Dad said. He then called out to Benjamin, "Come on in; Mortimer won't hurt you."

"Mortimer? Dad, where did you get a name like Mortimer?" I giggled as I tossed my knapsack on the dining room table.

"Mortimer the Mummy is his full name. I thought it was kind of cute."

"Dad, that guy is anything but cute. Can't you put

him somewhere else? Or at least dress him in a nice sweat suit?" I argued.

"Yeah, after dinner I'll do that. Now, go get that homework done," he jokingly said to me as my twin came in. They were talking as I went off to my room.

A couple of hours later, Dad called me for dinner. He isn't the greatest cook. Some parts of dinner were okay, but something he made was extremely salty. He called it his Dead Sea special. I knew what he was talking about, but Benjamin looked confused. Dad told him, "Ben, the Dead Sea is called dead because it has such a high salt content. Nothing can live in the water. In fact, there are so many minerals in the water that you can float in it without any effort."

After dinner I went back to my homework, but I was absolutely parched all evening. I think I drank about ten glasses of water. I was so thirsty that I even had to get up in the middle of the night to get a drink.

The light in the hall is connected to a big fan. The thing "needs a little work" as Dad says it. I say it just needs some oil. Anyway, I decided not to turn the light on because the fan would squeak and wake everyone up. Without a light, I felt my way through the black hallway. There wasn't even any moonlight. The sky is rarely clear where we live. It must have been a heavily clouded night because it was dark, I mean very dark.

I tiptoed down the hallway while I ran my hand

along the wall. Any minute now I expected to bump into Mortimer the Mummy. I wouldn't put it past Benjamin to have put extra salt on my food just to make me get up in the middle of the night. Suddenly, my fingers brushed some material. I slowly reached out until my whole hand touched a wrinkled prune face.

It was creepy to have this guy in my hallway. I knew that Dad said he was only a replica, but the ugly, wrinkled thing looked real enough to me. I'd been around Egyptian artifacts all my life. I knew that even if he was real, he couldn't hurt me. But still, I got goosebumps. The freakiest part was that I had never touched a mummy before. The replica's fake skin was stretched tight like leather over a skull. It sent shivers up and down my spine. Mummies, even fake ones, were definite spine chillers. I prayed as I moved my hand along his head, *Father, help me see things as they really are. I know that mummies can't come back to life, but my imagination sometimes gets away from me. Please take this fear from me.*

Knowing where the mummy stood in the hall gave me a peaceful feeling. I had touched it. I hadn't screamed, and now I could get my drink and go back to bed without embarrassing myself with any wild display of fear. I thanked God for keeping me calm.

I guided myself with my hand into the kitchen. Moving my palm along the smooth surface of the fridge, I came to the countertop. I was only inches away from the sink. The glasses were kept in the cupboard above it.

I reached up, popped open the cupboard, and grabbed a glass. Finally I could have that drink of water I needed so badly. I pushed the handle of the faucet upward to turn the water on, but my hand slipped. Water streamed full force into my glass.

It blasted into the bottom of the glass and then up the sides. It splashed out every which way. I jumped back to avoid getting totally drenched and crashed into something.

Whatever it was, it was not supposed to be there. I turned around to feel it. My hand touched a body wrapped in strips of material. Mortimer had followed me into the kitchen!

My mouth flew open and I almost screamed. Then I remembered that I was twelve years old and should be able to handle situations like this. I stumbled backward, this time to the sink. The hard spray of water still splashed out of the stainless steel sink, soaking the counter, the floor, and my pajamas. The cold made me leap forward. I didn't get too far. Mortimer was still waiting for me.

I started praying again. I needed my link with God. I needed to know that he was there with me. *Lord, I'm really scared this time. You've got to help me. None of this makes any sense. He's not supposed to be a real mummy. Besides, no one can come back from the dead except for Jesus.*

I quickly pushed myself off the cloth-covered creep and went sailing backward into the side of the sink. I rolled to my left to avoid the icy water that was spewing out. I reached over and smacked the faucet handle downward and shut off the water. One crisis taken care of.

But if Mortimer was wandering through our house like a bad nightmare, I needed to do something to protect my family. Before I did anything, I needed some light. I scooted my wet back along the refrigerator until I came to the wall with the light switch.

I flipped it on, but there was no light. Mortimer must have cut the electricity to the house! Instead of light, I heard a horrible grinding sound as if Mortimer were gritting his teeth to ready himself for his human meal. My mind raced. *What should I do next, Lord?* I prayed. The grinding noise was growing louder in my ears. Then it hit me, I hadn't turned on the light. It was the garbage disposal.

I knocked that switch down and the one next to it up. Light flooded my eyes, and I scrunched them closed. I slowly opened them. As they adjusted I kept on praying, *Father, please show me that this nightmare isn't really happening.* I shifted my stare to Mortimer. It wasn't him.

I started to laugh. Mom's Red Cross dummy was standing in the middle of the kitchen. She must have been practicing her bandaging techniques. It wasn't a mummy at all; it was my mom's dummy.

When a hand touched my shoulder, I screamed, "Ahhh, Mortimer leave me alone!"

"I'm sorry, Jessica, did I scare you?" Mom said. Dad stood right behind her with a big grin showing under his thick beard. I could see Benjamin behind them shaking with laughter. When I looked around

31

me at the puddled water on the floor, the Red Cross dummy, and my drenched reflection in the window glass, I laughed as well.

"I'm sorry about the mess, Mom. Dad's Dead Sea special made me really thirsty," I answered.

Benjamin stepped around Dad and looked at the floor. "Were you planning on lapping the water from the floor like a dog?"

"No," I shot back. "I just wanted a drink, and I didn't want to turn on the light and wake anyone up."

"A bold and brave concept, Jessica, but the light is on and here we all are. Since we're awake, we'll all help clean this up. We should be done in three shakes of a lamb's tail," Dad said.

"What does that mean, Dad? You say it all the time," Benjamin asked.

"Haven't the foggiest," he answered.

"What does that phrase mean? The foggiest what?" Benjamin returned.

"I believe it means that my brain is clouded, and if I get another question I may string you up by your thumbs," Dad responded with a big smile. Then he added, "I know, you want to know what that expression means. It was an ancient form of torture that I'm about to bring back."

"I take it that Benjamin's questions are a more modern form of torture," I quipped.

Mom interjected, "Ben, I really think we can take care of this. Why don't you go back to bed?"

Benjamin was more than glad to escape the labors of sopping up water from the floor. As he turned to leave the kitchen, Dad said to him, "Nighty night, sleep tight. Don't let the bed bugs bite."

"Dad, don't take me down that road or we'll be up all night discussing what that expression means," Benjamin said. My father laughed. Even in the middle of the night, I had great parents. *Thanks, Lord, for showing me how things really are and for the great parents that you've given me.*

We finished cleaning up, and Dad turned off the kitchen light as I got to my bedroom door. Somehow the dark wasn't as frightening as it had been.

As a kid, I used to imagine things were hiding in my room. One time I was sure there was a snake on the back of a chair near my bed. In the morning, when the first sunlight hit it, I saw that the snake was really a belt. Ghosts turned out to be white shirts hanging on hooks. There was always an explanation for my fears. It's always a help to know that the Holy Spirit is with me, especially when I'm afraid.

I yawned as I crossed the floor of my dark room. I was awfully tired. What should have been a five-minute thirst quencher had turned into a twenty-minute floor scrubbing. I thought how nice my warm, soft bed was going to feel.

I pulled back the covers and slipped into bed. I was lying on my back thinking about the crazy events of the last twenty minutes when I yawned a huge yawn.

It was definitely time to sleep. I rolled over to grab my teddy bear. I flopped my arm on the other side of the bed to feel for Teddy. I touched something, but it wasn't his fuzzy little body. There was no doubt in my mind, my arm was around Mortimer the Mobile Mummy!

I leaped from my bed to flip on the light. I was right. There in my bed, right where I'd expected to find Teddy, was the mummy.

I yelled as loud as I could, "Benjamin Hoffman, this means war!"

My parents were in the hallway in a second. Benjamin didn't make it past his doorway. He was crumpled on the floor holding his stomach from laughing so hard.

"I don't think it's funny, Benjamin," I spit out, as I glared his way.

I looked at my parents, and my mother was trying to stifle her laughter. "Mom, do you think what he did was funny?"

"Oh, it isn't funny right now, and I'm sure Dad is concerned about the mummy. But I just remembered something my brothers once did to me. One night I went to bed, and when I pulled back the sheets, I found a frog under them. I thought your uncles were all jerks, but I simply put the frog outside. What I didn't know was that they'd fixed up a tube that fed frogs into my bed about every ten minutes. I was furious then, but now, when I think of it, that frog story still makes me laugh. Then again, my brothers all found frogs in their shoes the next morning," Mom said.

"Mom, don't tell her that or she'll try to put Mortimer in my sneakers," Benjamin told her.

She turned to him and said, "You better get to bed. I want no more practical jokes tonight from either of you."

Dad chimed in, "And I'm not too happy about you moving the mummy. Even though he's a replica, Mortimer is fragile. I want you to refrain from using replicas of Egyptian antiquities as if they were rubber chickens." Then he scooped Mortimer out of my bed and carried him off to the garage where the old guy could rest without us living beings bothering him.

Mom let us sleep an extra fifteen minutes to make up for the half hour we lost the night before. Benjamin and I didn't talk much. I was still disgusted with his immature joke.

But by the time we got to the cafeteria for lunch I was over my irritation with him. We headed to our usual table where Becca and Adam already sat. As I sat down, I said to Becca, "I'm beat. My dad brought home a mummy last night, and it attacked me in the hallway, the kitchen, and then in bed."

36

Becca's eyes went wide with fear. She gulped and said, "It came to life? If the one at your house came to life, then the ones at the museum will too. I'm not sure I want to be a midnight snack."

Benjamin butted in, "What she forgot to tell you is that the mummy is a fake. She bumped into him in the dark hall. Besides, I put Mortimer in her bed."

"Cool!" Adam added. What fun Becca and I were going to have at the museum with those two refugees from an old horror movie.

"There's nothing to fear," Benjamin threw in. "Except for the curse of King Tut."

"The what? I thought that was only a fairy tale?" Becca said loudly.

Benjamin turned to me and asked, "Do you think we should tell them? I'm not so sure that telling would be a good idea. It could scare them and stop them from camping out with us in Tut's tomb."

"I think that should be their decision," I said through a smile.

"Please tell us. We've got to know," Becca begged.

"We've got a right to know if we'll be in danger," Adam added.

Benjamin sat back in his cafeteria chair and smiled smugly. "Well, okay, but the two of you have to promise that you'll go with us anyway."

"It's a promise," Adam said while Becca hesitantly nodded her head.

"There is a curse on King Tut's tomb. When it was first opened, they found . . ." The bell rang for us to go to our next class.

10

Becca and Adam were stunned when the bell rang. I wondered if Benjamin had planned it that way. I wouldn't put that type of teasing past him. Because the teacher in my next class didn't like us to come in late, I couldn't tell them the story.

The rest of the day went quickly, at least for me. When we stepped outside to wait for Dad to pick us up after school, Adam and Becca grabbed my brother.

"You have to tell us about the curse," Becca pleaded.

"I can't now. My dad should be arriving any minute," he teased.

"No, he won't," I said. "This morning Dad said he'd be about fifteen minutes late. So, I guess you have plenty of time." I knew that would keep him from teasing them any further.

Benjamin glared at me. He knew what I did to him. I smiled back to let him know that I did it on purpose as a little payback for putting Mortimer in my bed the night before.

"I really don't think there's enough time. This isn't some half-hour sitcom story. It's a made-for-TV-length story," Benjamin argued.

"Just start it then. You can finish it in the car on the way to the museum later," Becca said persuasively.

"All right, but when you're scared out of your wits and start shaking in the middle of the night, don't blame me," my brother said. Then he launched into the story of King Tut's curse.

"Twenty men and women were with Howard Carter and Lord Carnarvon when they opened the tomb of King Tutankhamen. No one knew if it would be filled with treasure or if it had been looted by burglars.

"When the group opened the tomb, they found the great treasures that you'll see tonight. At first the group was excited. Then Howard Carter found a clay tablet with hieroglyphics on it. Another one of the team, Alan Gardiner, translated the Egyptian writing. It was then that fear struck the archeological group. The inscription read: *Death will slay with his wings whoever disturbs the peace of the pharaoh.*

"Guys like Carter, Lord Carnarvon, and Gardiner weren't afraid of a curse, but they knew that their Egyptian workers would be. So they hid the clay tablet. In fact, all mention of its discovery was taken out of the records. No photos exist of it because soon after it was translated, the tablet disappeared."

"So, what's so scary about that?" Adam asked. "A tablet disappeared, big deal. Sometimes my homework vanishes—that doesn't mean that there's a curse of Adam."

"Are you sure that there isn't?" I kidded. Then I prodded my brother to get on with the story. "There's a lot more to the story, and it is scary."

Benjamin continued, "Within two months, Lord Carnarvon came down with a mysterious illness. He woke up one morning with a temperature of one hundred four degrees, and he was shaking with the chills. On the next day, he was feeling better. Then on the next day, the chills and fever came back again. For twelve days it went on: hot, cold, hot, cold, hot, cold.

"Then that twelfth night at one fifty A.M., Carnarvon died. Moments later, all the lights in the city of Cairo went out. What was even stranger was that Lord Carnarvon's dog died in England at the same time. The butler said that the dog began to howl, sat up on her hind legs, and fell over dead.

"There's more. Do you want to hear it?" Benjamin asked. Our friends stared at him and nodded their heads. Benjamin had them and he loved it.

"Arthur Mace took out the last chunk of wall that blocked the entry to the main chamber. Soon after Carnarvon died, Mace complained that he was getting more and more tired as each day went on. Suddenly, he fell into a coma and died. His disease was never diagnosed.

"George Gould, a friend of Carnarvon's, went to Cairo after he heard about the English lord's death. Howard Carter showed Gould around Tut's tomb, and the next day, Gould was dead.

"Then another man visited the tomb and returned to England, but the curse followed him there. He died mysteriously of a high fever. Another man, Archibald Reid, had cut the cords around the mummy. He grew very weak and finally died.

"Within six years, twenty-two people who had helped open the tomb or who had been connected to the Tut treasure had died. The strangest story was about Howard Carter's employee, Richard Bethell. One morning, he was discovered dead. When they told his father, the old guy died. Then, on the way to the cemetery, the hearse ran over a little boy."

I added to Benjamin's lecture, "Even the guy who wrote Sherlock Holmes said it was the curse that caused all these deaths."

"Wow, that really freaks me out. Do you think that the curse is still on the treasure?" Adam asked.

"I guess we'll find out tonight," Benjamin said mysteriously. Dad drove up, and we jumped in the car. Everyone was very quiet on the trip to the museum.

When we were almost there, Adam finally asked, "Benjamin, were you telling the truth about King Tut's curse?"

My dad overheard the question and asked, "Do you mean the one about all the mysterious deaths of anyone who touched Tut's stuff or the one about him walking around at night protecting it?"

Becca threw herself forward in the backseat, grabbed my dad by the shoulder, and asked, "Do you mean it's true?"

Dad opened his mouth to answer when a car horn sounded behind him and distracted him. "The driveway for the museum is the next turn up here," he said. Then he started giving us directions. "Once we park, grab your stuff out of the trunk. Stay near me so we can get cleared by security in one big group. Once we're inside, we can drop our things off by Tut's tomb and see some of the exhibits."

We went through the front door and headed straight for the tomb. There we stacked our things by the entrance to the exhibit of King Tut's final resting place. I knew it wouldn't be long until my father began his lecture tour of the museum. I had heard most of it many times before, but I knew that Adam and Becca were going to hear more than they could absorb.

We stopped in front of the museum's replica of the Egyptian Book of the Dead. Adam looked at my dad and asked, "What's that painted animal-like thing?"

Dad smiled and answered, "That is the Egyptian god Ammet. He's part crocodile, leopard, and hippo. To the left of Ammet you see a set of scales. Ammet's servants are weighing the heart of a dead Egyptian. If his heart is filled with good, he passes into the next world."

"Dad," I said, "it seems that every religion believes that God will judge people after they die. A lot of them teach that God will weigh their good actions against their bad. If you ask me, it seems pretty hopeless that most people could ever be good enough." I looked right at Benjamin.

"Do you see why we need a Savior then?" Dad asked.

"I guess so. The big difference between Christianity and other religions is that God doesn't weigh our good against our bad when we die. That's because of what Jesus did on the cross. He paid for all our sins, all our bad stuff," I answered.

In my mind I lifted up a quick prayer to God. *Father, your message is so different from the one the Egyptians lived by. Through Christ we have an entrance into heaven even though we don't deserve it. Thanks for that. I'm glad my heart will be weighed to see if Jesus is in it, not if I am good enough.*

Benjamin interrupted my prayer when he asked, "Dad, what are these little statues? Adam thinks they look like the toy soldiers we played with when we were kids."

"Not exactly, boys. Egyptians believed that when they died, they would have to work in the fields of the gods. They took these small figurines, called *ushabti*, into their tombs to do their service for them."

Adam chimed in, "I'll have to make sure that my action figure collection gets buried with me." We laughed at that as Dad led us into the prehistoric wing of the museum. Becca and I stayed right behind him, staring up at the dinosaur bones all around us. The two boys got distracted on the way and fell behind somewhere in the other rooms.

"Look how long that dinosaur's neck is. Dr. Hoffman, how do they keep those things from falling apart?" my friend quizzed Dad.

"Super glue," he said with a snorting laugh. "Just kidding. Can you see the cables coming down from the ceiling? They're pretty strong. They can support the dinosaur's weight and your weight and maybe even mine."

"Are these real dinosaur bones?" she asked. When he nodded, she said, "That is so cool. But if all we have are bones, then how do we know what they looked like with skin on them?"

Dad answered, "That's a good question, Becca. We don't know for sure, but we do know how muscles work. If you lay muscles over the bones and then skin over the muscles then it's pretty close to what you see in those pictures over there.

"Girls, this place is filled with our past. There are a lot of answers to age-old questions standing right in front of you." As he pointed out another skeleton, his lecture was interrupted by a panicky sounding yell. Was that one of the boys?

We ran back toward the Egyptian exhibit. I looked to the left and Becca looked to the right. Dad hurried around the tomb of King Tutankhamen. None of us saw a thing. Where was Adam? Where was Benjamin?

"Ben, where are you?" my father yelled.

"Right here, Dad. Why all the yelling?" my twin brother said as he slipped from the entrance to the tomb. "I was just getting some gum from my knapsack."

"Where's Adam?" I tossed at him.

"The last time I saw him, he was heading toward the Egyptian jewelry exhibit," Benjamin answered.

When we got to the jewelry room, Adam was standing in front of an open case that displayed an amulet.

"Did you yell, Adam?" Dad asked.

He looked a little sheepish. "Actually I got lost and wondered where you were. I'm curious about the curse. I mean, who gets it? What killed off those people in Egypt?"

"Supposedly anyone who touched the artifacts from Tut's tomb would die," Dad answered. "As for the stories of the people who opened the tomb or touched the artifacts and later died, many of the deaths were a little more natural than the stories lead us to believe."

Adam looked at my dad and pointed to the amulet in the open case. "What do the markings on this necklace say?"

Before dad could answer Benjamin bumped into Adam and caused him to touch the edge of the arti-fact. He jerked his hand away with a startled look.

My father looked at the necklace, then explained, "All the objects in the museum have note cards next to them. They explain what the piece is. The card for this one was damaged and is being replaced. This is an anulet. It was used to ward off evil. It belonged to King Tutankhamen."

"Who?" Adam said with a gulp.

"King Tut, and now you've got the curse," Becca said as she edged away from him. "Do me a favor; stay away. If a high fever strikes you, don't spread it. If a mummy comes after you tonight, let your mummy tuck you in while we get away."

"Dr. Hoffman, you can't get the curse from, like, touching a piece of Tut's stuff, can you? Mummies listen to reason, don't they? He wouldn't come after me in the middle of the night, would he? And if this stuff is so dangerous, why isn't this glass case sealed?" Adam asked with real fear in his eyes.

"Well, Adam, this case isn't sealed yet because the top was broken earlier today when it was being set up. Before the museum opens tomorrow the museum staff will put the glass top in place so no one will catch the curse," Dad told him with a half smile.

I couldn't resist teasing Adam. As he listened to my dad, I slipped quietly behind an Egyptian casket next to the glass case. It was easy enough to get behind Adam without him seeing me. As he fumbled for words, I reached out and gently touched the back of his neck.

"Ahhhhhhhh!" he screamed. I had never seen anyone's hair stand on end before. Adam was too frozen to turn around and see who or what had touched his neck.

The moment he saw the others laugh, he figured out he wasn't in danger and turned around. "Jessica, please don't do that to a guy who just got zapped with one of the world's most ancient curses."

Dad continued laughing as he strolled from the room. Becca, Benjamin, and I followed after him. We left Adam standing with his mouth wide open as he backed slowly away from the glass case.

I giggled some more when I heard him softly say to the case, "Nice Tut. Good Tut. I only accidentally touched it. See, it's totally, completely undamaged. Be a good mummy and don't come and get me."

Adam suddenly realized that he was alone again with the artifacts that King Tut had sworn to defend. I heard him come tearing through the room. His sneakers smacked the floor hard. Without looking, he turned the corner sharply and came face to face with the one thing he did not want to see—a mummy.

Adam hit the brakes hard and fell as he screamed, "Dr. Hoffman, King Tut is after me."

When we came into the room, Adam was on the floor. The mummy had tipped over on top of him. Its head had torn off and bounced along the museum's hard floor. It ricocheted off the wall across from us.

The arms also fell off. One of the mummy's hands covered Adam's eyes as the body pinned him to the floor.

Adam's face projected terror. My dad reached down to pull the mummy off our friend. As Dad's hand touched Adam's elbow, Adam let out a howl that echoed throughout the halls of the Shield Museum. He squirmed desperately to escape. "I'm sorry, Tut. I'll never touch your junk ever again."

"Junk?" Dad questioned with surprise.

"Junk, treasure, whatever you want me to call it, that's what I'll call it. Just let me live," Adam pleaded fearfully.

"Adam, will you open your eyes? It's me, Dr. Hoffman."

He slowly opened his eyes and gave a weak smile. "I knew it all the time. I was just kidding around. Real funny, wasn't it?" Adam said. Then he continued sorrowfully, "I'm sorry, Dr. Hoffman. If I broke anything, the museum can take it out of my allowance."

"Adam, if this were a real mummy and not a museum replica, your allowance would take close to a century to pay it off," my dad said.

I moved in closer and asked with relief, "It isn't real?"

"No, it's a demonstration model. The museum guides use it when they're giving tours to show how different parts of a mummy were prepared for mummification. It's supposed to come apart. Adam's lucky that his carelessness didn't cause a real disaster," Dad explained. Then he shook his head and pulled Adam to his feet. "I think it's time to get the four of you into your nice, safe sleeping bags inside Tut's tomb."

"Couldn't I sleep out in the car or something?" Adam asked.

Becca and I moved closer to him, and each of us grabbed an arm. We guided him toward the opening to Tut's tomb. After a few steps, when he was walking on his own, Adam stopped and picked up what looked like a jewel from the floor. "What's this? Is it a piece of broken glass or something?"

My father picked it out of Adam's hand and stared at it in the dim light. "This isn't from a mummy display. It looks like a jewel from some ancient work of art. It must have fallen while the piece was being transported. That's unusual, though, because the museum staff is so careful. Somebody must've been in a big hurry. Adam, you've gone from nearly destroying a display to possibly saving one. Good work. I'll make sure the museum curators get this tomorrow."

"Dad, do you think that it was those jewel thieves that I read about?" I asked.

"Honestly, I don't know, but I doubt it. The museum security is very tight. I don't know how someone would get in," Dad answered.

"An inside job," I remarked.

"A what?" Becca said.

"An inside job. If you can't get in after the museum closes then it would have to be an inside job, someone who works here," I answered.

"Earth to Jessica. Not everything in this world is a mystery. Quit playing FBI," Benjamin said.

I have to admit that I'm a mystery fanatic. I love trying to solve them.

Dad motioned with his head, and we followed him into the replica of the pyramid. He stopped us for a second and spoke in a soft voice, "Before you settle in for the night, I want to give you a little tour of what's inside while I arrange some of the pieces. I'm sure that none of us will ever get another chance like this again. Ask questions about things because I may start talking like an Egyptologist. Feel free to interrupt me."

We strolled down the ramp that led to the antechamber and Dad began, "Tut was known as the boy king because of how young he was when he came to the throne. He was only eighteen when he died. It's amazing that his reign had so little impact on the Egyptian dynasties, yet he's the best known of all pharaohs. All that you'll be seeing in the next few minutes is the reason for his notoriety. Just think, when he was your age, he was the leader of his nation."

"Dad, how did he do it at this age?" Benjamin asked.

"Lots of good people helped the young pharaoh make decisions," Dad answered as he led us into the next room. I found myself talking to God as we walked. *Father, I don't think I'd want to be president or pharaoh at my age. I'm glad things are the way they are. Thanks for giving me a life like this.*

The antechamber held Tut's chariot so he would have something to travel in while he's in the great beyond. In one corner of the room stood Tutankhamen's ceremonial chair.

Becca asked, "What does the high-ro-gyro stuff on the chair say?"

"Hieroglyphics, Becca. They're a series of symbols for different sounds and sometimes for words. For instance, this cross that has a loop at the top is called an *ankh*. That's the sound it symbolizes, but in certain sentences it also translates as the word *life*. This says, 'Tutankhamen, ruler of Thebes, King of Upper and Lower Egypt: Lord of Two lands, Nebkheperura, given life. Son of Ra whom he loves. May the good god live, likeness of Ra, the protector of the Ruler of Heliopolis, the king who is clear sighted like Thoth and who is fair of face.' It goes on with more wonderful descriptions of Tut."

Benjamin butted in, "They'll probably say all that stuff about me on my tombstone." We all acted as if he hadn't said anything.

Dad pointed to a square a few feet away and continued our Egyptian education. "That is the Golden Shrine. The writings on it say much the same thing as on the throne. There's also an ostrich feather fan against the wall. Everything around us are things Tut and servants would have used.

"The annex," he said as he led us past two tall, thin lion statues and into the next room, "was filled with baskets, chairs, vases, cups, plates, and other household items for Tut to use in the next life. I guess his eternal home didn't come furnished." No one else got Dad's joke, but I giggled to myself.

We backed up and passed through the antechamber

again to the burial chamber. Tut's mummy had been encased in three caskets. To the right of the burial chamber was Tut's treasury. Dad explained what each piece was. We were surprised to see how much gold and how many precious jewels were used to decorate them.

"Dr. Hoffman, isn't it dangerous to have all this gold and jewelry where people can get to it?" Adam wanted to know.

"The museum is safe. Usually there are guards in here, but this evening we're here. These areas are also usually roped off and wired with alarms. But since part of my job is to arrange some of this stuff, the museum curator turned the inside alarms off. In the morning, I'm sure guards will search each of us as we exit. Who knows? One of us could be the world-famous jewel thief," he said with a grin. We all looked at each other suspiciously and started giggling.

As we moved on to another piece, Becca slipped. Her hands went up to grab onto any nearby solid object to get her footing. She pulled away a basket that kept a spear lodged against the wall. It slid along the wall and came crashing down only inches from the unsuspecting Adam.

He looked at us and said in a faint voice, "It's the curse." At the same moment, an electric candle on the ledge above him dimmed and brightened and then went out.

14

It couldn't be the curse. I didn't believe in it. Dad didn't believe in it. In fact I planned to prove it didn't exist this very night. But no matter what I said to myself, at this moment it looked like there really was a curse. My heart beat like thunder, and my mouth dried up like a cracked river bed. I prayed for the Lord to calm me down.

"I think that we've seen enough tonight," Dad said, as he put the basket and spear back in their places. "Let's head back to our sleeping bags and grab something to eat. Then I'm going to take a crack at some of the museum's hieroglyphics." The thought of being left alone seemed to terrify Adam, and it secretly put me into a near panic. I was beginning to think that I preferred the kind of mysteries you find in books, not the kind that you live out.

"Do you mean that you won't be with us all night?" Adam asked my dad.

"I'll just be in another part of the museum for two

hours or so, but I brought our walkie-talkies from home. They have fresh batteries, so we can be in contact at any time if necessary," he answered.

Adam sighed with relief as we wandered back to our ancient Egyptian campsite. I had decided to stay awake all night with the walkie-talkie in my hand. When we got to the gear, each of us unrolled our sleeping bag. Dad got dinner together. It wasn't the kind of stuff that you get on a real camp out. There weren't any hot dogs or marshmallows, but the place where we ate it made up for any lack of warm food.

We formed a circle and talked about school. Benjamin was trying to keep the subject light so Adam wouldn't get upset, but Adam brought the curse back to the center of our conversation. "Dr. Hoffman, where did all this stuff about curses come from?"

"Curses written on clay tablets have been found in several tombs of the ancient Egyptian kings. One read, 'The spirit of the dead will wring the neck of a grave robber as if it were that of a goose.' Two corpses were inside that burial chamber. One was the king who was mummified; the other was a grave robber whose skull had been crushed. A stone fell from the ceiling just as the robber had reached out to take the mummy's jewelry."

"Wow, just like in those Indiana Jones movies," Adam said with surprise.

"Why did they believe in curses in the Egyptian days? They were pretty advanced in a lot of ways, weren't they? It seems odd to me," Becca said.

"They were advanced. But to the average uneducated Egyptian, the pharaohs seemed like gods. The kings used this to keep their people under their power. Later, when even common people learned more about the calendar, math, astronomy, geometry, and irrigation, the kings were in a position to lose their power over the people. So, they manufactured tricks like a falling stone to frighten robbers and make them believe in the curses. It was the belief in the curse that was supposed to keep grave robbers out of the tombs. The curses didn't do such a great job. Most tombs had already been pillaged by the time our archeologists discovered them," Dad told us.

"I think that really stinks," Becca said.

We all looked at her with that what-are-you-talking-about blank stare. She felt obligated to explain her statement. "Those kings took all that money from their people and then buried it with themselves. That must have kept most of the families at poverty level while the kings lived like . . ."

"Royalty?" Benjamin offered.

"Yeah, that is exactly it," she answered.

"It isn't much different from countries today where there are dictators in power. Do you think they live in shacks just like their people?" I asked her.

"Well, it still stinks," she repeated.

Adam wasn't ready to let the conversation about the curses die. But I wanted to change the subject. It only reminded me how scared I had been earlier. Adam asked my father, "Did anyone else die from a curse besides those around King Tut?"

"Sure, some archeologists went crazy and some died of mysterious fevers, but we can't blame a curse for all those situations. It could have been an unknown disease at their time that is as simple as the flu," Dad answered. "Why don't you guys turn in now? I need to get to my work so I can get some sleep tonight as well."

He stood up but lost his balance and fell against the wall. I leaped to my feet with Benjamin right next to me. "What's wrong, Dad?" I asked anxiously.

"I seem to be getting a fever and . . ." he said as he fell to the ground.

15

Benjamin yelled, "Dad, are you all right?" With my cold sweating palm I reached out to Dad.

"Benjamin, get some water," I ordered. My brother hurried to his canteen and carried it back. I tried to pour some down Dad's throat with my shaking hand when I heard him chuckle. "Dad," I said in a scolding voice. "Why did you do that?"

He got to his feet and said, "That's what things would look like around here if there were such a thing as Tut's curse. By now one of us would be experiencing that weird fever, but as you can see, it hasn't happened to me or to any of you."

Benjamin butted in, "Dad, didn't someone else die from that weird disease after visiting the tomb? And what about that guy from the museum that died?"

"The story is that he was unpacking some of the artifacts from Tut's tomb and dropped dead in the museum." Dad stopped and glanced at his watch. "I need to get to those hieroglyphics. So, let's get settled in."

"What killed the museum worker?" I asked with a shaky voice.

"I'll explain it while you get into your sleeping bags and get comfortable." As we started to snuggle in, Dad continued, "Lots of things can happen to someone to make him drop over dead on the spot. The worker could have had a heart attack."

Adam was chewing on a stick of licorice, and Dad looked right at him when he added, "He could have choked on something that he was eating." Adam coughed. We all laughed. He was right, it could have been as simple as that, but with everything else that happened to people who touched Tut's stuff, we were still a little frightened. Maybe the mystery of a curse wasn't a good thing to try and solve.

I found myself praying, *Father, I am so scared. I'd rather just leave, but I know that we can't. I want Dad to stay with us, but I know that he can't. You will have to teach me how to lean on you when I'm scared.* My fear lessened as I reminded myself that God would be with us.

My father scooped up his briefcase and turned to leave. He looked back at us and said, "I'll be downstairs in one of the storage rooms. I haven't seen these writings before, so I don't know how difficult they'll be to translate. So, the four of you lie down, don't touch anything, and go to sleep. I'll be back before any mummies can tuck you in."

I was feeling much calmer. As Dad left, I looked at Becca and she smiled back. We had something planned to scare the boys once they were asleep.

I started the plan off by saying, "Dad is right. I think I'll curl up in my bag and go to sleep."

"That's a good idea, Jessica. I'm going to do the same," Becca responded. We lay down and winked at one another. I reached up and turned off my flashlight. There was a dim security light, but Benjamin's flashlight still cast a glow on the pyramid's inner walls.

"Maybe we better get some sleep too, Benjamin," Adam said, but I could tell from the fake way he said it that they were up to something. I wasn't about to fall asleep and let them play a trick on me.

We all lay there for about fifteen minutes. I had grown more tired by the second and was starting to doubt that I could stay awake long enough to pull off our joke on the boys. I must have fallen asleep because I woke to the sound of a voice.

"Jessica, you have violated my tomb. My curse is on you. I am coming to get you. I am taking you to my home in the nether world."

I wasn't scared. I knew it was Benjamin and Adam. I sat up in my sleeping bag. Standing beside me was a pretty sorry-looking mummy. Adam had wrapped

Benjamin in Mom's first-aid class bandages. I covered my mouth with my hand to keep from cracking up, but Becca started to giggle. Soon all four of us were laughing hard.

As we stopped to catch our breath, we heard a noise like feet scraping across the floor. "That's enough, Dad, we know you're out there," I called.

Silence.

Then we heard the sound of something being dragged across the floor.

"If it isn't your dad, who's making those noises?" Becca asked.

Adam gulped and said in a high-pitched voice, "Tut?"

We looked at each other. I could see the fear on my
friends' faces. We were the only ones in the museum.
My dad was working downstairs, and none of us
could have made the sounds. *Lord,* I prayed, *What do
I do now? We're scared. I'm sure that Daniel was
frightened when he was in the lions' den, but you protected him. Protect us too.*

We needed to do something. "I'm going to go find
out what's making noise out there," I whispered as
softly as I could. I didn't want my voice to give away
my plan. Before I could leave the group, Benjamin
touched my arm. He was unwinding the bandages as
fast as he could.

"Sis, I don't think you should go out there alone,"
he said.

"Does that mean you want to come with me?"

"No, it doesn't mean that. I'm not sure any of us
should go out there. Besides, it could just be a
mouse," he told me.

"An awfully big mouse," Becca said doubtfully. Then she stiffened her body to give herself strength. "Jessica is right. Someone has to go out there. If she's going, then so am I." Becca slipped out of her sleeping bag. Together we stepped toward the doorway. We heard two more sets of steps behind us. The boys were coming too.

I stuck my head out of the entrance. I couldn't see anything moving, and the sound had stopped. "Whatever it was, it seems to be gone. Maybe we better go out there and take a better look."

Benjamin softly responded, "When we walk out, Becca can go straight ahead and check the room over there. Adam turn to your left and slip along the wall over there. Jessica go to the right. I'll go around behind the pyramid. If Tut is out there, one of us will see him. When you do—scream. I don't think any of us want to tangle with Tut by ourselves."

Each of us nodded our heads in agreement. Becca and Adam crept out first. The museum had grown darker. The dim lighting made everything harder to see. Most forms were misty silhouettes. I couldn't tell what they were until I was nearly on top of them. Fortunately, none of them turned out to be Tut. That was a relief.

I circled around the room being as quiet as possible. I still heard nothing, and I hoped that nothing heard me. My steps were soft, but on the hard floor it was nearly impossible to creep along without making some noise. I turned the corner and crossed in front of a mummy. Was it real or another model? I couldn't tell in the dark. I stared at it and held my breath. If the linen-wrapped body was Tut's, then I might be joining him in the great beyond. But there was no movement.

Clink! It sounded like a small metal object had fallen to the floor. I looked away from the mummy to see where the noise had come from. Then I looked back quickly. I was sure the mummy had shifted its weight to the other foot. But I was also sure that this mummy could not walk the earth. It must have been my imagination.

Imagination or not, I was so scared that goosebumps popped up all over my body. The hair on the back of my neck prickled. I wasn't sure that I liked this type of mystery. It was a little too real.

I turned the corner and headed toward where I heard the metal drop. After a few steps I could feel the presence of someone else in the room. My heart started pounding in my throat. *Father in heaven, please help me! Take this fear out of me, and save me from anything evil here.* I was spinning around to see who was there when a hand grabbed my arm. I opened my mouth to scream, and Becca stepped in front of me.

She whispered in a frightened voice, "Sorry to scare you, but when you walked in, I thought you were a mummy. To be honest, I'm scared, really scared."

Softly I told her, "So am I. It looks like there's nothing here. We should head back to the pyramid and see what the boys discovered."

We retraced my steps to the pyramid. When we came around the corner, something looked different. For a moment, I couldn't put my finger on it. Like a bolt of lightning, the realization went off in my brain. The mummy I saw before was gone!

I pulled Becca to a dead stop. "I don't want to scare you any more than you are, but when I was coming into your room to see what fell, I walked by a mummy. It was standing right on that platform. He isn't there anymore."

"Are you sure?"

"Yeah, I'm sure. As sure as I know you dropped something metal in your room," I responded, trying to make my point without raising my voice.

"Then he wasn't there, because I was also heading toward that noise. I thought you dropped something," she exclaimed, raising our fear several notches. I could feel cold sweat on my forehead as my breath came in quick gasps.

We turned and scanned the room, but in the darkness just about everything looked like a monster. In another second we bolted for the pyramid entrance and went diving inside to where our sleeping bags were.

"Grab your flashlight, Becca. We need to get some light in the dark corners and shadows," I ordered. Both of us dug through our bags, but neither of us found flashlights.

Becca gave me a puzzled look and said, "I know that I left mine in here. I saw it just before we left."

"Then Tut's been in here. He's probably heading to the caskets below. We've got to go find the boys," I told her. We leaped to our feet. I was almost out the entrance when I crashed into a figure coming in.

I would have screamed except that Benjamin said something before I could. "Jessica, what's going on? I heard you running to the pyramid. Did you see something?"

"It's what we didn't see," I told him. "First I saw a mummy, and then it was gone. A second ago we were looking for our flashlights, and we can't find them anywhere. We think Tut has been here and taken them. He could be in the burial chamber right now."

"Do you think that we should go down there and find out?" Becca fearfully inquired.

"I guess so," my brother told her. Adam screamed for help. Tut had him! We froze with fright.

I forced my fear-paralyzed body to move and was on my way out of the pyramid when Becca jerked on my arm. She looked at me and insisted, "Wait a second. We can't go running out there and into Tut's hands. We need some kind of plan."

Benjamin pushed by us both, saying, "He's my best friend. I don't need a plan to help him. When we get out there, you two keep Tut occupied while I free Adam."

"That works for me," I said while I prayed for God to help us. Benjamin led the charge out of the pyramid, but we stopped outside. "Which way do we go?"

Becca yelled, "Adam, where are you?" Then she looked at us and added, "That ought to give us our answer real quick."

The next few seconds were deathly still. We heard nothing. My face went into a heavy frown. Then Adam's voice called back, "Near the front door. Hurry, I'm in trouble."

We ran across the floor toward the door. I saw nothing. Then out of the corner of my eye I noticed something moving. I heard a grunting sound. "Adam's in the goldfish pond near the front door," I reported.

In another second we were standing over Adam. "You're lucky this pond has been drained for repairs. How did you get in there?" Benjamin asked.

"I'm not really sure. I thought I saw something move in this area and I walked over. Believe me, I was scared, but I hoped the movement was only my imagination. When I got to the edge, I looked in to see if our friendly neighborhood mummy had gone for a swim. As I bent over, I felt something push me," Adam told us as Benjamin and I reached down and clasped his hands. Before we yanked him up, I wanted to know more.

"Did you see the assailant?" I asked. The others looked at me like I was crazy. I said, "That's what the cops always say on TV."

"We're not cops, and we're not on TV," my brother reminded me. How I wished we were in a TV mystery show and not in the middle of the terror of Tut.

Adam cut off my response by answering my question. "I'm not sure. I thought I did. As I fell I looked back but only for half a second. I saw this big thing, and it looked like it was wrapped in strips of cloth."

"Quit kidding," Becca cautioned. "I'm scared

enough already." She helped as Benjamin and I pulled Adam's body over the edge of the pond.

He looked her in the eyes and said, "I'm not kidding around. That's what I saw. I'm just as scared as you are, Becca, but I can't deny what I think I saw."

There was no doubt that Adam was telling the truth. He certainly could kid around, but this wasn't one of those times. He was as serious as I've ever seen him.

"What do we do next?" Adam asked.

"Find Dad," I said.

"We can't," Benjamin spit out quickly. "If you remember, we're locked in on this floor and he's in the basement. We can't get out of here without setting off the exit alarms."

"What about the walkie-talkies?" Adam asked.

That's when I remembered I hadn't seen my walkie-talkie where I'd left it by my sleeping bag. Tut must have taken it along with our flashlights. "Tut took it. We can't get hold of Dad. We're stuck here with the living-dead." There was something strange about ancient mummies taking flashlights and walkie-talkies. How would they even know what they were?

"Should we stay near the pyramid?" Becca asked.

"We have to get everything we need to protect ourselves out of the pyramid. I'm not sure it's safe to be that near his burial chamber with all his treasure down there," my brother cautioned.

"But his stuff is everywhere," Adam reminded us. "No matter where we go, we'll run into an exhibit of his things. If Tut is going to protect his treasure then he'll do it everywhere in this building. We're doomed no matter which way we go." He sounded like he was speaking from under a big, black cloud.

"We're only doomed if he catches us. Let's grab our things and see if we can find a safe place to hide," I said. I started the walk through the dark museum room back to the model tomb of King Tutankhamen. None of us said anything as we walked, but I could tell what was on everyone's minds. How do we survive the night? I turned to God as we marched through the high-ceilinged room. *Father, we're in big trouble. David often prayed for your protection while in battle, and you gave it to him. I'm asking for the same thing. Protect us from our enemy.*

We were halfway across the room when we heard a deep, echoing laugh coming from behind us. We spun quickly but didn't see a thing until Becca pointed her finger and said, "A shadow."

Moving along the wall was an elongated and distorted shadow. It would have been hard to tell who or what it was except for a long strip of material hanging down behind the image on the wall. We'd all seen enough monster movies to know what it was. Unfortunately, I couldn't turn off this video. This was for real. This monster movie script had been written with us as the stars, or maybe as the victims.

Adam broke ranks and headed toward a display of Tut's jewelry. Benjamin whispered to him, "Where are you going?"

"I just remembered the amulet that your dad said was worn to ward off evil spirits. I think I'd like to have it around my neck. Our mummy friend might recognize it and not come near us then," he said.

"Don't forget, it's part of Tut's stuff," I warned.

"Everything is part of King Tut's treasure. But if that amulet can do the trick, then I'm willing to try it." Adam stated, as he walked closer to the case where the amulet was lying.

"Please don't pick it up. It doesn't seem right to wear ancient treasure. I wish we could just get out of here," Becca said tearfully. "I don't think I like this museum or mummies or King Tut or sleepovers. I want to go home."

"We all do, but we have no choice. We can't get out, and we can't let the mummy get us. We need to be strong and support each other," Benjamin told us. "Let's get our stuff out of the pyramid. We'll need every possible weapon in our arsenals." My brother sounded like a general telling his soldiers what to do next. "I guess you're right. We need to put our trust in God, and not in some ancient necklace," Adam said, as we all fell in behind Benjamin and marched to the pyramid.

We went inside and froze. It looked like someone had gone through our knapsacks and sleeping bags again. Our things had been thrown around the room. The sacks were tipped over, and stuff was missing.

"It looks like the mummy doesn't want us to leave this place. I guess our mummy is no dummy. And we're left with absolutely no weapons," I glumly reported.

"Not true," Becca added. "Remember when we were down in the treasure room and a spear almost hit Adam?"

"I remember the experience quite well, but how can that help?" Adam said.

"If there is one spear in this pyramid, there must be other weapons. We only need to find them, and then we'll have something to defend ourselves with," Becca answered him with an encouraging smile. Even though we were all stiff with fear, I saw glimpses of courage in each of us.

"I hate to break your bubble, but what good is a spear against a beast that's been dead hundreds of years? I think we'd only make him mad at us," my brother told us. It was something that I hadn't thought of before.

"Let's just find a safe place to hide until Dad gets back," I told them.

Before the others could agree, we heard something fall deep within the tomb, and the sound echoed loudly. Our eyes darted from one to another.

I felt like I was frozen in my spot. I had become a statue of terror.

Then something else fell, and it sounded closer. Greater fear freed us, and we started backing toward the door. The not-so-dead dead guy was somewhere inside the pyramid. The same pyramid that we were inside. Something fell again. Only this time the sound came from the museum room behind us.

Becca whispered through her dry throat, "If King Tut is inside the burial chamber, then who or what is outside?"

The others were sure that I was crazy when I broke into a smile and exclaimed, "That's it!"

"What's it?" my brother asked with surprise over my glee.

"Becca and I were on the other side of the museum, and I was sure that I saw a mummy. But when I walked past that spot later, it was gone. There must be two of them," I said.

"That's two too many for me," Adam added.

"Wait a second. We have two mummies? Can someone tell me why Jessica is so happy? I think one of us ought to think of a way out of this mess," Benjamin lectured.

"Okay, Benjamin, go ahead and tell us what we should do," Adam told his best friend.

"I don't know. The only thing that we have left is our sleeping bags. What good would they be against a mummy?" he responded.

"None," Adam tossed back.

"Hold it! I just got an idea. What if we zipped two of the bags together? We could use them like a net and wrap up one of those wrinkled pharaohs," I suggested.

Everyone agreed. We grabbed two of the bags and attached them. As we did, I asked the others to pray with me. "Jesus, we're fighting something unknown. I don't know if we're doing the right thing, but I ask you to protect us. Send your angels ahead of us so we can defeat our enemy." We said "amen" together, then Adam and I each took an end of the doubled sleeping bag. When we heard the mummy in the passage, I looked back at my brother and whispered, "Are you ready?"

He nodded his head. I quietly counted to three, and Adam and I raced with the bag between us. In the dim light of the museum room, I couldn't tell what was waiting for us, but I felt the sleeping bag catch something. We continued pulling, but the weight of our catch slowed us down. Finally our captive fell. "Thank you, Lord," I yelled out loud.

Adam and I dropped our ends of the sleeping bags and tore off toward the room opposite the pyramid. I glanced back over my shoulder to see where Becca and my brother were. They ran from the pyramid entrance and leaped over the lump under the sleeping bags.

The four of us skidded along the slick floor of the

dark room until we were safely behind a large exhibit. Becca breathlessly leaned into the center of us and asked, "Did you see anything before the sleeping bags got our monster?"

"Not a thing," Adam told her.

My answer was different. "He was big, but I'm sure it was a mummy. I only saw him for a second," I reported.

"How do you know it was a mummy if you only saw it for a second?" my brother asked.

"I thought I saw the head wrapped up. That's about all I could see."

"Then we're not sure what's out there?" Benjamin said.

"Well, it isn't Jaws. What do you think is out there? We're in a museum that has all of King Tut's worldly possessions, and he put a curse on anyone who touches them. We've all seen something that looks like a mummy. So, what's left to believe? You've got to examine the clues. As much as I don't believe in those things—I have to face the facts," Adam argued. He sounded cranky.

"Okay, Adam, you win. You're probably right, but it's just so hard to believe," Benjamin said.

"Believe this, I think I just heard something coming our way," Adam warned. We all sat still and waited. It sounded like soft feet were shuffling along the smooth floor. We ducked behind an exhibit as two shadows came toward us. The mummy we snared must have gotten free. They seemed to be gathering parts of Tut's treasure. The two mummies never saw us, and they continued out of the room. We all sighed.

I motioned for the others to follow me. Something had caught my eye for mystery. I wanted to find out where the mummies were going. My greatest worry was that the mummies would come back for more treasure as we were heading their way.

My brother touched my shoulder and said, "Jessica, this hallway leads to the back of the building. There's no place to hide back there. If they came this way then we have a good idea what the mummies plan to do with the treasure. I just don't want to see what they plan to do with us."

He was right, and I knew it. I smiled and said, "I want to see what's around this corner. Then we'll find a safe place to hide. Agreed?"

They nodded their heads in agreement. We took three steps and stopped again. I stood at the corner but was afraid to turn it. Maybe our mummy friends were only inches away.

Before I moved I whispered a little prayer. *God, I hope I'm not about to get us all into big trouble. Be with me.*

I stuck my head around the corner. In the darkness of the hallway, I couldn't tell at first if there was anything there. My eyes adjusted quickly and I could see that the hall was empty. "It's clear, but I can see several doors."

I was into the hallway to explore it before the others could remind me that I said I'd turn around after I saw beyond the corner. The first door said MAINTENANCE on it. The next one read ANTIQUITIES OFFICE. When Adam read that, he looked at Benjamin and asked quietly, "Is that like an antique store?"

"No, I think it must be the office for people who study old things. That's what antiquities are. It's old stuff that old guys like my dad study," Benjamin answered thoughtfully.

"I was hoping it was like a gift shop. I wanted to get my grandmother something," he told us.

"I don't think this is the time to think about shopping. If we don't think of a way to protect ourselves or find a place to hide, none of us will be doing much shopping in the future," Becca scolded.

Without warning, the door swung open. We were staring into the dark, dead eyes of King Tut. He growled with a horrible, vicious roar. Then two linen-wrapped hands filled the air in front of us. He was reaching for us.

Adam ducked and barely escaped the mummy's grasp. By the time the mummy swung his cloth-wrapped arms at us again, we were racing back down the hall-way. Benjamin took a sharp left and then another. We had entered a huge room. I brought my sneakers to a hard screech and looked around. From the sound of things, the mummies weren't too far behind us.

I yelled to the others, "Operation Jonah." They stopped and gave me an inquisitive look. Then they saw the large replica of a whale that ran along the right side of the room. Everyone knew right away what I was telling them to do.

Adam was the first to jump the rope around the exhibit and squeeze behind the whale. He was edg-ing his way along the dark wall as Becca, and then Benjamin, followed him. As I slid into the narrow passage between the whale and the wall, Benjamin asked, "Jessica, if we knew what you meant by 'Operation Jonah,' then don't you think Tut and his pal will know too?"

"I don't think they're Bible-toting, Sunday-go-to-meetin' kind of guys. Let's just get hidden and let them pass us by. I think we'll be safe here for a little while," I responded.

I had barely pulled my feet behind the giant mammal when our unwelcome visitors crossed the threshold of the room. We could hear their cloth-covered feet scurrying along the floor.

Adam inched closer to Benjamin and whispered, "Benjamin, give me a hand. I want to see what they're doing." My brother cupped his hands, and Adam stepped into them. Benjamin raised him in the air until he could peer over the big whale.

Becca tilted her head up to whisper, "What do you see? Are they still out there? Are the mummies getting closer to us?"

He didn't answer her. I was glad because I was sure his voice would carry across the room and draw their attention. I needed time to think over the clues up to this point. Who had dropped the jewel? Why would the mummies go into an antiquities room? Why would they take our flashlights and walkie-talkies?

I had hoped we could hide behind the whale until my dad came back. I realized that I was very tired. I yawned. Unfortunately, when I yawn, I often stretch without thinking. My hand smacked into the rope surrounding the whale exhibit. The brass pole holding it up tipped. I shot my hand out to grab it, but it was just out of reach.

Lord, this could mean disaster to us. Please don't let it fall over, I prayed as I frantically stretched to catch it.

Becca noticed me grabbing for the pole. Her face had fear written all over it in capital letters. She motioned with her hands and mouthed the words, "No, not that. Anything but that."

CRASH! BOOM! The pole fell to the floor, and my outstretched body followed right behind it.

Adam's voice cut through the echoes of the crash. "Thanks, Jessica, I think they know where we are now. I should add, too, that they are heading our way as fast as their little rag slippers will move."

Adam called down to us, "The mummies are getting close to our hiding place, but I have a plan." He jumped down and filled us in. The moment the mummies started squeezing in through the narrow opening between the whale and the wall, my brother yelled, "Now!"

With cupped hands, I threw Becca into the air. She flew over the tail of the whale and landed on the floor. Then I did the same with Adam. There were only seconds left, and my brother was racing in my direction. He leaped, placing his foot in my hand. I threw his body into the air. Benjamin landed next to Becca. He scrambled back to the whale and reached his hands over the thinnest part of the whale. "Run and jump up to me. I'll pull you over and the other two will catch you." I moved backward to get a running start. My right foot dug into the floor. I was ready to make the best jump of my life when the linen-wrapped fingers of King Tut touched me.

The mummies growled. I looked over at my friends and yelled, "Pray!" I thought my knees were going to buckle, but our prayers were answered. I got a sudden burst of energy and strength. Before Tut's hand could wrap around me, I was racing toward the tail of the whale. I leaped into the air, grabbing at my brother's hands. He caught me and flipped me over the top of the whale. I came down in the arms of our two friends.

We were all glad that our middle school had gymnastics in our phys ed classes. Our leaps put us safely out of the reach of our enemies.

We ran out of the room looking back to see how close Tut was. The two mummies were struggling out from behind the whale. Their tangling linen wrappings gave our escape the extra minutes it needed.

Once we were out of sight and sound, I skidded along the linoleum and pointed ahead. "There is our hiding place."

"Where?" Becca asked.

"The *shaduf*," I responded.

"All I see is a big bucket over a pool of water," she said shaking her head like I was crazy.

"*Shaduf* is what the Egyptians call that big bucket. That one looks big enough for us all to hide behind. They'll never find us there," I encouraged the others. I waved for them to follow me. Holding to a rope, we crossed the narrow walkway above the pool of water until we could drop on to a ledge behind the *shaduf.*

Once we were safe, Adam whispered, "What's this thing called again?"

Benjamin answered for me since he was closest. "It's a *shaduf.* You say it, 'shad-oof.' And my sister is right. They'll never think to look back here."

Becca gave me a serious look and said, "I was wondering. Let's say Tut played hide-and-seek when he was a little kid before he got to be king. Couldn't he have hidden behind a big bucket like this? And if he did, don't you think he'll look for us behind this one?"

"I don't think hide-and-seek was invented back then," Benjamin said.

"This isn't a game of hide-and-seek. It's more like a game of hide-and-shriek," Adam popped in.

"It still isn't logical," Benjamin said.

"When did Mr. Spock join us?" I asked him.

Becca put her finger to her lips to quiet us down. We could hear the familiar sound of cloth-wrapped feet shuffling across the floor. King Tut was still far enough away that none of us were worried. But as his footsteps grew closer, we began to worry.

We were afraid to say a word. The sounds came closer, and we heard the mummy grunt. Then the bucket shook. It felt like the undead beast had grabbed the rope and was coming toward us on the walkway.

I tried to remember how long the walkway was. The mummy wasn't moving very fast, but each tug on the rope told us he had moved a little closer. In another minute, the mummy would discover us.

I began to imagine what would happen. Since the *shaduf* was a demonstration exhibit, the mummy could drop the bucket into the pond. We would probably fall with it since we only stood on a thin ledge. That would make us easy to snatch from the water, like the rubber duckies in that children's carnival game.

Lord, it's me, Jessica. I think we're in big trouble once more. Is there anything you can do? I prayed quickly.

Becca was moving around. She pushed on the bucket lightly. My best friend looked at the rest of us and whispered as low as she could, "When he is close enough, we have to start rocking the bucket. With a little luck, it will knock him off the walkway and into the pond."

"I wonder what will happen to him if he gets wet," Benjamin said.

"I hope he melts like the witch in the *Wizard of Oz*," I snapped.

The mummy's hand appeared on the edge of the bucket, and Becca yelled, "Now!" We all threw our bodies toward the bucket and then pushed back to the wall. The *shaduf* moved slightly. On our next shove, it began to rock. By the fourth one, the *shaduf* had gone into full motion, but we hadn't heard the splashing sound that we expected.

Adam scrambled from behind the bucket and then slid back. "It worked," he told us. "Except the mummy kept himself from falling in by grabbing some of the exhibit-stuff in the pond. He won't be able to catch us if we cross the rope now."

"Where's the other one?" I asked.

Adam shrugged his shoulders to say that he didn't know. That concerned me. We could escape from one and fall right into the hands of the other mummy. But I knew we couldn't stay behind the *shaduf* any longer. I led our charge from behind the bucket and grabbed the rope. We moved quickly along it until we could drop to the edge of the pond.

The moment my shoes hit the floor, I was running. I hadn't gotten far when Adam screamed. I turned around just as the mummy's free hand reached up from the pond and latched onto Adam's ankle.

The rest of us turned quickly, but no one was close enough to break the freak's tight grip on our friend. I felt helpless. We had been so close to escaping, and now Adam was set to be the mummy's midnight snack. I could see the pain on Benjamin's face because he wasn't able to help.

When I looked at Becca, she was no longer standing next to us. She had jumped up and grabbed the rope. My friend was heading back toward Adam. I wasn't sure what she had planned, so I watched very closely in case I could help.

Becca was about a foot from Adam and the mummy. She started to swing her body back and forth, bouncing on the rope. Adam and the mummy bounced with her. The mummy could barely keep his balance. If Adam let go then both he and our visitor from another century would tumble into the water.

Becca's acrobatics on the rope became more intense. Finally she made one last swing and kicked her feet toward the mummy's hands. The speed of her kick gave Becca's impact with the mummy's tight grip real power. The once-dead and now not-so-dead guy let go of Adam. The mummy caught himself before he slipped into the pond. But by the time he had regained his balance, the four of us were racing across the floor.

While we ran, Adam said, "Thanks, Becca. I was sure I was toast back there." He panted and asked, "Does anyone know where we're going?"

Benjamin pointed ahead to a long boat. "That *senusert* is at least forty feet long. There will be plenty of room to hide in it."

Senuserts were used by the Egyptians to travel along the Nile River. This one would make a really good place to hide. When I saw it earlier in the evening, I thought about the trips down the river Egyptian royalty would have taken in it. Now I saw the big boat in a completely different light. Instead of wondering about the people it must have carried hundreds of years ago, I was thinking about the four people it would carry in a few minutes.

The museum had made it into a demonstration exhibit. A staircase usually stood near it so visitors could climb inside. But I didn't see the stairs earlier when we walked by it, and the boat was too high for us to jump into without some help. While we ran, my eyes darted from one side of the boat to the other in hopes of finding a ladder, a chair, a stool, or even a table we could use to reach the edge of the boat.

I spotted something. Standing at the foot of the boat was an Egyptian statue that had the head of an animal and the body of a man. From another visit to the museum I knew it was only a copy. It looked easy to climb on, and once we reached its top, we could jump into the boat.

When we got near the boat, the statue seemed out of place. I looked at the floor and saw scratch marks. They made me suspicious, but I assured myself that they were most likely made by the people who installed the exhibit. It probably wasn't some clue I should be concerned about.

I was the first to scramble to the top of the statue. I stepped into his outstretched hands, onto his shoulders, and then on the top of his head. I reached the boat's edge easily and pulled myself inside.

The boat's sides cut off the little bit of light in the room. Even if a mummy looked inside the boat, he wouldn't be able to see us. The darkness was a good cover. I thanked God for something as simple as the darkness, but a verse kept trying to come into my mind. It was something about darkness.

"Hurry up," I heard Adam say to one of the others. He was right. We had very little time to hide before the mummy would be close once again. I heard Becca's voice getting near me. She must have been the one that Adam told to hurry. Then I heard her gasp. That was followed by a thud. I poked my head over the side to see what had happened.

Becca had slipped down the statue and landed safely but frustrated at the bottom. She quickly grabbed onto the half-beast, half-man statue and climbed up toward me. The delay gave me a bad feeling. There would only be a matter of minutes before one of the mummies would see us. While I watched the others, something about a verse and the darkness haunted my memory.

Becca got closer again, and I held my breath, hoping she would make it. In the quiet I became aware of something else. It wasn't very loud, but I was sure my ears were picking up the sound of someone breathing. That breathing wasn't far from me. At first I thought one of the others had somehow gotten inside the boat. My second guess was that the second mummy was inside with me. Suddenly, that verse came to my mind. How could I have forgotten it? It was only three verses away from my favorite one, John 3:16. In verse 19, the apostle said, ". . . They wanted darkness because they were doing evil things."

I began to feel like the dark *senusert* wasn't as safe as I thought. When a linen-wrapped hand grabbed me by the back of my sweatshirt, I knew that my second guess had been right.

94

I screamed as loud as I could, "Run, there's a mummy in here, and he's got me. Get away before he gets you!"

I listened to their feet race away from me. My mind bounced from one escape plan to another. I knew I had saved my friends, but I needed to figure out how to break free and save myself. The dark inside of the boat made it impossible to see anything.

God, please get me out of this. If you do, I promise to clean my room up every day and never complain about going to church or Sunday school, I bargained with my prayer. It was a desperate prayer; I knew that God didn't bargain. If he saved me, it would be because he loved me. It certainly wouldn't be because of anything I could do for him.

Some of the mummy's linen wrap started coming loose. I could feel it as he tried to move me inside the *senusert*. I pulled from side to side in an attempt to break free. Nothing worked.

The mummy's size and strength won, and he dragged me through the boat by one arm. I kept feeling for something to hold on to with my free hand, but it came up empty time and time again. I was surprised that this mummy didn't smell all musty like the other mummies I had been around.

For some reason, I thought that should be a clue. Even in all my fear, the detective in me was searching for clues. Unfortunately, I wasn't sure what the mystery was. All the clues seemed to point me toward something, but a good detective never solves the mystery until all the clues are gathered. Things aren't always what they look like.

I pulled at the loose strip of linen. The piece got longer. There had to be something I could do with it.

My mind felt empty of possible ideas or possible ways to escape. In a few minutes it would be too late. Suddenly, an idea hit me. That loose cloth was wide enough to cover the mummy's mouth and nose. I hoped it was thick enough to make it hard for the mummy to breathe. All I needed to do was get both hands free so I could wrap it around and tuck it in behind his head. By the time he freed himself, I could be climbing down that half-man, half-lion statue.

I let my body go limp. The mummy became confused and loosened his grip on me. I dropped to the bottom of the boat, and the creepy guy leaned over me. I grabbed the tail of the cloth, wrapped and tucked it before he could stop me.

He went for his face, and I immediately went for the end of the boat. I was there and over the side before I even heard his feet stumbling through the ancient wooden boat.

I ran away as fast as I could. When I turned the corner, I stopped and leaned over to catch my breath. After sucking air deeply into my lungs, I remembered that my friends and I were separated. I stared all around me. There was no sign of them. I was glad that they had gotten away, but I was afraid. I didn't want to be alone in Tut's exhibit while the king roamed the rooms to get vengeance on anyone who touched his stuff.

I moved slowly, keeping my back to the wall. In the dim light, I prayed for the ability to see anything dangerous before it saw me. On the other side of the Egyptian exhibit was a doorway that led to the dinosaurs. There were at least a dozen real dino skeletons and a few models made to look like the real thing.

I slipped into the corner behind a glass case filled with ancient jewelry and precious stones. I felt like I'd been in phys ed for ten days straight, all day and all night. I knew I needed to crouch low to the floor, and my tired muscles were more than glad to go limp.

I listened carefully but heard nothing. This was my opportunity to creep into the dinosaur room, but first

I sat still to pray. *Lord, I know that I bargained with you before, and that wasn't right. Thank you for warning me of danger through your Word. I promise to listen harder to what you're telling me. Right now, Lord, please help me find my brother and friends.*

I began creeping along and was able to stay close to the wall until I came to a stone sarcophagus, the outer stone casket that held two inner ones. As I looked at it, I realized it would be a great place to hide because it was made of stone and was totally indestructible. But I decided not to try it. I could never have moved the heavy stone top by myself. The dinosaur room was the best hiding place for me.

I left the safety of the dark wall and tiptoed around the big casket. I rubbed my hand along its edge as I made my way toward the dinosaur room. I was halfway along the sarcophagus when two hands reached out of the stone burial vault and grabbed me. After working so hard to escape, I was captured again!

I tried to pull away from the hands. I twisted and yanked my body, but nothing worked. I clenched my free fist to punch the beast and turned to look at my target. It smiled at me. I had seen that face many, many times before.

"Be quiet, Jessica, or you'll wake up all the mummies," Benjamin said to me. Next to him, looking at me from inside the sarcophagus, were our two best friends. I sighed and smiled at them.

"I was just thinking that the sarcophagus would be a great place to hide. I can see that we're all starting to think alike," I whispered.

Becca broke in, "I don't like that."

"That I found you?" I questioned.

"No, that isn't it. I don't like that you thought this would be a great place to hide and so did we. It makes me think that the mummies might also think of it. If we're inside and they know it, they could easily trap us by adding weight to the top. We can barely move it now. I vote that we look for a better hiding place."

"Becca is right. If they figured out the boat and were waiting for us, then this sarcophagus could end up being *our* burial vault. I was heading for the dinosaur room. There has to be a less obvious place in there," I answered.

"Why don't we just try to break out of here?" Adam inquired.

"The moment we do that, all the exit alarms will go off. Then the mummies will hear them and slip back into their tombs. The cops will come in, and they won't believe us. They'll think we're crazy. We've got to keep from getting caught and wait till it's the right moment to capture them," Benjamin instructed.

"That's a good idea. Once we have them, we can tell our story and have living, well, *once-living* proof that we're telling the truth. That's why I chose the dinosaur room. The mummies know everything about the Egyptian places to hide, but they don't know anything about dinosaurs. Maybe we can trap them in there and then call the cops," I suggested.

"What do we catch them with?" Adam wanted to know.

"We won't know that until the three of you get out of that box and we all get to the dinosaurs. Let's get moving." I was already two steps away from them when I said it. The others leaped from the old stone casket and fell in behind me.

Suddenly, I heard a distant growl. I looked at Benjamin and saw that his face had gone pale. Adam's and Becca's showed a mix of fear and disappointment. The sound had to have come from one of the mummies. I whispered, "We can't go into the dinosaur room yet. I don't want them to know our plan. We need to divert them."

"There's the gift shop," Becca pointed out.

"This is no time for shopping," Adam told her.

"I need to pick up a few things for someone very close to me, my mummy," she joked, but none of us stopped to laugh. We ran into the gift shop entrance.

All four of us scanned the large gift center. I saw almost nothing we could protect ourselves with. *Lord, help!* I thought. Then I looked at the shelf down the last aisle. There I saw a stack of inflatable mummies. I had an idea. If we could blow up a dozen of those, the mummies might be scared or at least diverted by their own images. The sample stood nearly six feet tall. It was perfect to scare off our visitors from the nether world.

I pulled one out of the box and realized that it would take a long time to blow it up. I was staring intently at the plastic mummy when Becca tapped me on the shoulder. I turned and looked at her. She reminded me of a little kid. In her hand was a bunch of helium balloons. In a flash it hit me. We could blow up the mummies using the helium tank. Not only would it work fast, but a dozen plastic, floating mummies could frighten any person, living or dead.

I grabbed the others and told them my plan. We each took an armful of the inflatable toys and carried them to the helium tank on the other side of the gift shop. When the first one was filled, we let it go. The weight of the plastic kept the toy from floating to the ceiling. It hovered and drifted about a foot off the ground.

It didn't take us long to fill all twelve of them. We stood looking at our handiwork when Adam added a suggestion, "What if we put T-shirts or sweatshirts on four of these and tuck them behind the others? There are all kinds of shirts here. The mummies will waste at least ten minutes fighting the floating mummies to get to us. Or at least what they think is us. We can hide in the front of the store and run out once they're distracted."

Everyone liked the idea. We each chose a shirt from the racks and dressed a floating freak. Then we grouped the other helium mummies together in front of the four dressed like us. The dim store lights made the glorified balloons look very scary and mysterious. After we finished, we went to the front of the gift shop and hid behind the checkout counter. We made it there in just enough time to hide. The mummies entered the store a few minutes later.

Something bothered me. Where had the mummies

been while we were blowing up the inflatable copies of them? That was another clue. I knew it, but I didn't know what it meant.

Their wrapped and withered bodies wandered along the shelves knocking different toys and gifts on the floor. We could hear things fall to the floor with loud crashes. Suddenly everything went quiet. Then we heard a loud roar. The mummies had found their plastic images.

We could hear them thrashing their way through the helium balloons. We shot from our hiding places and ran toward the dinosaur exhibit.

As I leaped over the counter, I looked back to see the mummies struggling through the inflatable figures. All I could see was a sea of plastic images bouncing around the room. I smiled and turned toward the door, but my smile turned to shock. I was staring into the face of a mummy!

I nearly yelled but caught myself before it escaped from my mouth. My twin brother was right behind me, and he gave the mummy a shove. The helium-filled figure floated out of our way. That had been a close call. If I had screamed, the mummies would have been on our trails too quickly for us to hide. I didn't even let the others know how much the mummy had frightened me.

We ran quickly and quietly to the dinosaur exhibit. The linen-wrapped visitors from ancient Egypt were nowhere near us. We could talk freely and make our plans.

Becca pointed up to the head of a brontosaurus and started giving us all orders. She was like a drill sergeant in a movie. "Jessica and Adam, climb to the top of that dinosaur on the scaffolding that's around it."

"The brontosaurus?" Adam asked.

"Yeah, the whatever. I don't care right now if it's a

brontosaurus or a buckin' bronco. Once you're up there, find what you can to toss down. It looks like there's something up on that platform," she instructed.

"Will it support our weight?" I asked.

"Sure, it will," my brother reassured us. "The scaffolding is built for climbing. It looks like museum workers have been making repairs to that guy's head."

Becca pushed us toward the structure surrounding the huge skeleton. Before I took my first step up I asked, "What are you two going to do?"

She answered, "Benjamin and I will attract the mummies. They'll chase us under the dinosaur. You drop whatever you find up there on their heads. When we've knocked the mummies senseless, we can set off an alarm to get the police here."

Her plan sounded great except for one thing. I was afraid of heights. "Do I have to go all the way up there?"

Benjamin knew about my fear. "It makes the most sense. Becca and I are the fastest. If you two miss, then we still have a chance to escape, but don't you dare miss. Tut can have his gold and jewels, but I don't want him to have any of us."

My twin was right. I resigned myself to deal with my fear of heights. I'd discovered it when I'd visited the world's tallest building with my family. We had taken an elevator to the observation deck and walked over to the windows. The closer I got, the heavier my feet became. The last thing I wanted was to look out over Lake Michigan and the city. I forced myself to the railing near the window. I gripped it to hold myself up and then looked out. That's the last thing I remember about the building. My head began to spin, and I slipped to the floor. Fortunately, Dad was there to catch me, and Mom used her first-aid skills to revive me.

I wasn't sure what would happen now, but I knew I had to climb up beside those bones. I had to help save us all from the monsters chasing us.

The first few steps up the scaffold didn't frighten me. Once I cleared the first level around the leg and started to shinny up the pole by the rib cage, the fear started. Each movement upward made a shiver run down my spine, and my breath came in fast, short gulps. The boat was only eight feet tall, but this was at least twice that, or more.

Father, I don't know if I can do this. I'm scared to climb, and I'm scared not to climb. Help me, I cried out to God.

Adam was right behind me. He didn't seem scared, and he didn't notice how scared I was. He encouraged me as we climbed higher.

"Jessica, we ought to write a book about this when we're done," he told me as he scooted up past the rib cage.

106

"I've thought about that, but who in the world would believe it?"

"I would. I wouldn't have believed it before, but I will never doubt another bizarre ghost story again," he whispered.

"I'm still not sure about our mummies, Adam. The clues don't all add up to them being visitors from the ancient past. Besides, I just don't see any proof from the Bible that this sort of thing can happen," I told him.

"That's the part that bothers me. I've got to ask the youth pastor about some of these things when we get out of here. That is, if we get out of here. How much farther do we have to go?" he asked.

I looked up. "I think I've got another few feet, and then the hard part begins. We have to balance ourselves on that narrow plank until we reach the neck."

"Good, the neck won't be hard. That part of the scaffold looks like a ladder," he said positively. I wished that my mind could agree. All of it seemed hard. I got to the top of the scaffold around the rib cage and pulled myself onto my stomach. I lay on the thin board that ran along the spine of the brontosaurus for a few seconds to catch my breath. The next part really scared me. *Lord, help me. I'm terrified of what I've got to do next.*

I pushed myself up to my feet. It was only seven steps to the neck. But once I was on my feet, my heart started pounding loud enough to attract the monsters from as far away as the pyramid. I lifted my arms and held them straight out at my sides to help me keep my balance.

The first step went fine. On the second one my foot slipped slightly. It wasn't enough to make me fall, but it was enough to cause my head to spin. I had to make it to the neck ladder quickly or I would fall. I was sure of it.

I knew I had to race along the board to the neck. The spinning increased in my head. I made up my mind that I had to do it. Without another thought, I ran for the ladder. Steps two, three, and four landed solidly on the thin, wooden walkway.

Step five was a different story. My left foot struck the edge of the board, and my ankle turned. I lost my balance and started to fall to the side. In an instant I planted my right foot and dove for the ladder-like scaffold around the neck. I reached out and grabbed for it, but the dizziness had already made me weak. My grip was loose, and I started slipping. Soon someone would have to scrape me up off the hard floor. I squeaked out, "Help!"

The shock of almost falling must have jarred away the spinning circles that chased around inside my head. Suddenly, I had enough energy and presence of mind to grip the scaffolding with all my strength. That gave Adam the extra few seconds he needed to race across the thin pathway to the bottom of the neck. He reached over and latched onto my hand.

"Don't worry, Jessica. A friend is always willing to lend a hand," he said just before he jerked me up next to him.

"Thanks, Adam. I forgot to tell you that I hate heights. I think I'll be okay now. Something like nearly falling to my death always clears my head," I said. Then I nodded to the neck-bone ladder ahead of us. "We better get up there before Becca comes up here and carries us up."

I went ahead of him so he could keep an eye on me. In a few minutes, we made it to the plywood platform by the head of the brontosaurus and started looking for heavy things to drop down. We found a couple of plaster bones someone had prepared to repair the dinosaur. Sometimes archeologists don't find all the bones when they dig up a dinosaur, and the gaps have to be filled with plaster bones.

I motioned to Becca that everything was ready. It was time for their end of the plan. Becca and my brother went to the doorway and yelled, "All right, mummies, we've had enough of you two. Come in here and we'll fight it out." They stood watching for the refugees from the sand dunes of Egypt's ancient past to discover them.

Nothing happened. We all watched for a sign of them. Nothing. Benjamin screamed, "Hey, mummy, why don't you come in here and tuck me in? I'm ready for you. Come on, tuck me in, mummy!"

There was still no sign of them. All night long mummies had appeared when we didn't want to see them. Now that we were ready for them, the creeps wouldn't cooperate.

Then two silhouettes appeared against the windows of the next room. The strategy had worked! King Tut and his aide came sliding into the room toward Becca and Benjamin. When the two ancient Egyptian hit men were close, the kids took off running. Benjamin was the first to run beneath us. I was tempted to pay him back for all his practical jokes and let a plaster bone drop on his head, but then I'd have to carry him home.

Becca was inches behind him. That meant our targets would run past us soon. Adam and I waited patiently, well, as patiently as we could while sitting on a brontosaurus head with plaster bones in our hands.

The larger of the two, Tut's aide, crossed under us first. He made an easy target. *Lord, guide this hunk of plaster.* I let go of the bone in my hand. My timing was perfect. The piece of plaster jawbone struck the mummy directly on top of the head. He pitched forward and sprawled across the floor.

Adam readied himself for the second mummy. Tut saw what had happened to his aide and tried to stop. The boy king slowed just enough so that Adam's bone bomb dropped an inch in front of Tut.

The monster from the past jerked his head upward and looked at us. Then he bent over and stared at the plaster bone that Adam had dropped in front of him. His eyes went back to us before his feet moved toward the brontosaurus's leg and the scaffolding. King Tut was coming for us, and Adam and I had no way to escape. *Father, listen, I really enjoy praying and all that. But at this point I'd rather not have so many terrifying things happening to me. Help me, Lord.*

As we perched on top of the scaffold, we watched the mummy climb toward us. In a few minutes, Adam and I would be on the floor next to the plaster bone I had tossed down. There was no mystery about the fact that Adam and I were in trouble.

Our mummy friend had made it up the scaffolding to the ribs of the dinosaur. It wouldn't be long before he reached us. We had nowhere to climb. We had no escape. I watched the dirty, cloth-wrapped creature pull itself up one foot at a time. Tut threw his leg over the thin board along the spine of the brontosaurus. His next move was to stand and inch our way.

But his linen wrap was slick. He fell to the board, straddling it with one leg on each side and kicked around in the air trying to find a place to hold on. He mumbled something. It must have been Egyptian, but it sounded just like the word *ouch* to me.

He steadied himself and tried another approach. Raising himself up on his knees, he tried to creep along the narrow wood. The linen around his knees and hands slowed him down.

He slipped a second time but grabbed the lowest bone on the neck to keep himself from slipping to the floor. Using his arms, he pulled himself along on his belly. I couldn't believe he made it to the bottom of the ladder.

Tut stepped on the first rung and then the second. I watched as he climbed several more. I touched Adam's shoulder and whispered, "This all sounded like a good idea when Becca thought of it, but I don't think it worked. Where are they? We could use some help right about now."

I spoke a moment too soon. I looked down and my brother was looking up at us. I yelled to him, "Benjamin, help us!"

He scrambled around the floor looking for something to throw. He spotted the two plaster bones Adam and I had thrown down. He picked one up and tossed it with all his strength in the direction of the mummy. His aim was close, but the bone bounced off the scaffold inches in front of Tut. It made the boy king move backward, and one foot slipped. He dropped to the rung below and steadied himself.

I prayed that Benjamin's next toss would smack the mummy in the head and knock him to the ground. It wouldn't be easy. As Ben reached for the other bone to throw, Adam called down to him, "This one has to do, Benny buddy." Then Adam started baseball chatter to encourage my brother. "C'mon babe, toss it up here, babe. You can do it, babe. C'mon, Benny ol' buddy." It sounded funny, but if it would help my brother knock our mummy off the dino scaffolding, I would've grabbed pom-poms and cheered him too.

King Tut stopped and held on tightly. All three of us waited for Benjamin's next pitch at the Egyptian king. *My Lord, guide his throw like you did mine.*

Benjamin reared back and swung the fake bone from deep behind his back. It soared into the air. His throw was perfectly on target. The bone hurtled through the dimly lit room higher and higher. In a few seconds, our mummy would be a dummy.

The bone was only a foot from his head. I braced myself to watch the impact of the dino bone on Tut's ancient skull. Then the mummy's hand darted from its hold and snatched the piece of flying plaster out of the air. Our last hope was erased like an error on a test. *Oh no!*

"What now?" I asked Adam. I was sure he could hear the panic in my voice.

"I don't know."

I thought I heard Tut laugh. The *ouch* and the laugh got tucked away in my mental clue file. I was getting closer to my answer. I was deep in thought when he began to climb toward us again. I moved to the far edge of the plywood platform and hung onto the thick cable coming out of the ceiling. Adam scooted closer to me. We had no room left to move. King Tut had won this battle, and obviously he had also won the war.

Tut came closer, and Adam and I clung to the support cable. I noticed that when Adam moved, his weight made the scaffold sway a little. I did it on purpose and the platform moved more.

I leaned my head in close to Adam's ear. I didn't want our visitor from the burial vault to get any idea of what we were about to do. "Adam, when Tut reaches up to grab us, he'll have to let go with at least one hand. If we start rocking the scaffolding from side to side then, we might be able to shake him loose."

Adam looked at me with his face beaming. He believed my idea would work. Tut was as close as he could get on the ladder. His next move had to be to reach for us. The mummy kneeled and tentatively reached up. He wasn't the bravest mummy that I had ever met. Of course, I could have been wrong. I haven't really met that many mummies. Then it hit me. Why would a mummy act like he's afraid of heights. He shouldn't have been afraid to die—he was already dead. Wasn't he?

His arm stretched out, and Tut was off balance. Adam and I rocked the scaffold. Tut teetered. We rocked harder, and the dinosaur's neck began to sway from side to side as well. Through the slits over the mummy's eyes I saw his first look of fear. Then he pitched to the side, desperately grabbing at the air. He toppled off the scaffold.

I closed my eyes. I didn't want to see Tut crash to

the floor. In the silence, Adam said, "Jessica, open your eyes. His wrappings are caught on a bone. He'll be up here for a while, so let's get down and call for help."

I popped my eyes open and saw Tut dangling by his own wrappings of death. His arms and legs were kicking in the air as he tried to get himself close enough to some part of the dinosaur or scaffold to grab on to. It looked impossible. One mummy was out cold and the other was hung up. *Praise God!* It was time to show the world the truth behind the curse of King Tut.

As I climbed down the scaffolding, I thought of what I would say to the newspaper reporters. I wanted something witty like, "I said tah-tah to Tut" or "That mummy was a dummy."

Adam and I dropped to the floor and looked for the other two. They were nowhere in sight, but the second mummy was still on the floor. I walked over to him. I wanted to touch him while it was safe to do so. The clues were adding up. We had found a jewel lying on the floor in the museum. The mummies' grave clothes didn't smell like other mummies I had been around. One mummy was afraid of falling. Both of them were definitely evil and loved the darkness.

I kneeled next to his head and leaned over. I put a hand on his head to roll it over so I could see his mummy-wrapped face. I expected to see all the wrinkles of a raisin showing from the eye slits. They weren't there. Had this mummy had plastic surgery?

I turned back to Adam to tell him to come and look. My head only turned a fraction when I felt the hard, tight grip of linen wrappings around my arm. Sleeping Beauty was awake.

"Ahh!" I screamed. Adam wasn't looking my way until he heard me. He had to hurry. The mummy was awake enough to hold on, but I don't think he could stand yet. I had to get free, and we had to get out of the room. I tried to jerk my arm away, but I only helped to pull the mummy up from the floor. I couldn't see Adam. If he couldn't come up with a plan to save me, I was toast.

The creep from the crypt pushed himself up with his free hand. Then I heard the distinctive sound of sneakers slapping on the floor. I knew it was Adam, but I couldn't see him.

Suddenly, out of the shadow cast by the towering dinosaur skeleton, Adam came flying through the air. He screamed so loud that the sound bounced from one wall to another. The mummy rolled over to see what was coming his way.

The moment he looked into Adam's face, my brother's best friend snapped on one of our high-powered flashlights. The sudden bright light blinded the mummy. He instinctively covered his eyes. That was all the time I needed. I was twenty feet away from our ancient enemy before he realized that the light was off and his prey was gone.

Adam and I made it to a far corner of the room. We turned it and expected to find a long hallway. We were wrong. We'd found a door. For the third time in the last few minutes we were trapped by the mummies.

Heavenly Father, all my life I've heard the great stories from the Old Testament. I know all the ways that you protected your people. I'm not asking for the dividing of the Red Sea or anything, but we need you to protect us. Just like you protected your people in the Old Testament.

"Any suggestions?" Adam asked. He sounded defeated.

"Run for it. That's our only hope. We have to run right by him and then find Becca and Benjamin. There's safety in numbers, and I don't think two is a high enough number for this game," I told him. Then a question struck me. "Adam, where did you find that flashlight?"

"Not-so-dead guy number two had something in his hand when you beaned him with the plaster bone. It landed a few feet away from him when he fell. I went over to see what it was, and I found one of our flashlights. Maybe the mummies got scared of the dark," he answered.

"Adam, why would mummies be afraid of the dark or even need a flashlight to see? Something really bizarre is going on around here," I told him.

Adam nodded and said, "I know, but one of the mummies is awake and waiting for us. Let's lay some shoe rubber and get out of here." I didn't even have time to answer or think about the flashlight again before Adam took off running. I wasn't about to wait for another invitation. I shot out of the little nook at full speed. I ran through the room expecting to see the mummy that grabbed me. He wasn't there. I looked up at the brontosaurus. King Tut still dangled from his wrappings.

I couldn't tell if Adam knew where he was going or if he was simply running to get away. I decided it was best to stay with him, no matter where he headed. In another few steps it became obvious that Adam had headed back toward the pyramid.

I panted out as I pulled up alongside him, "Do you think Becca and my brother are back at the pyramid?"

"I hope so. If they're not, I don't know what to do."

I looked up and realized a mummy had somehow gotten ahead of us. It looked like he planned to cut us off at the pyramid.

"I think there's been a change of plans," I yelled to Adam.

"You're right. Let's go!" We dug in our heels and quickly spun back around toward the dinosaur room. I had a feeling that neither of us knew where we were running to. We just knew who we were running from.

I remembered how hard it had been to see Adam when he raced through the shadows under the brontosaurus. I pointed in that direction. We cut to our right and flew by the dinosaur's tail. In the next instant, we were under the bronty's belly. I glanced back. The mummy was gaining on us. It seemed strange that he could suddenly run so fast. Even stranger, his running steps sounded like shoe leather hitting the floor and not linen wrappings. I knew that was another clue, but he was about fifteen feet away and I didn't have any more time to think about it.

Adam nudged me and pointed. Above us, Tut started to unravel. With each kick, a little more wrap came loose, and he spun farther down like a yo-yo. When we ran under him, Tut's aide was only a few feet away.

The aide leaped at us, and I heard a terrible scream from above. I didn't need to look to know that Tut was dropping in on the party.

I jerked my head to see how close the mummy was. I was just in time to see the last of Tut's wrappings come loose. He dropped another ten feet and landed right on top of his aide. They crashed together in a heap on the floor. My heart jumped for happiness. God had stopped our enemies, just like he promised. *Thank you, Lord. I really can trust you all the time and in every situation.*

I stopped to stare. It took me a few minutes, but I realized there was something wrong with Tut. In the dim light, I couldn't make it out, but I was also too frightened to get any closer. I'd already nearly found out that this type of mummy's hug could kill you.

I stood motionless, staring at our two buddies from ancient history. Benjamin and Becca startled me by blasting through the doorway.

"We're back and the police are coming," Benjamin told us quickly. He looked around the room for our attackers. Then his eyes fell on the two "floored" and wrapped Egyptian packages. "What happened to them?" he asked.

"Our modern, superior intellect outsmarted the two of them," Adam reported.

"Yeah, we convinced one of them to fall on the other one," I said, then paused. I looked down at the boy king and said to the others, "What's really strange is how Tut looks. It's hard to see in the dark, but I think we've solved the mystery of Tut's curse." I looked around the room for the flashlight Adam had saved me with earlier. "Adam, where's that flashlight you found?"

"I dropped it over there," he said and directed us near a skeleton of Tyrannosaurus Rex. Even without skin over his bones, T-Rex looked big and scary. "Help me find the flashlight. Don't anyone go near the mummies until we've checked them out with the light. Jessica was grabbed by one of them, and I had to risk my life to save her," he added as we searched.

After a minute, I heard a noise and asked, "What was that?"

"The police must be here. Great! They'll have a flashlight, and they can take care of Tut and his companion," Becca answered.

Benjamin sat back and wondered, "What can the police do? Give the mummies life imprisonment?"

"Let's find out," Adam told us. He stood up and turned around. His eyes went wide.

I had to look even though I knew what I'd see. Benjamin, Becca, and I leaped to our feet at the same time. We turned and saw two silhouettes standing in the dark shadows of the brontosaurus.

We spread out to give them a harder target to catch. They also separated. Tut's aide moved into the red light of the exit sign. It made him look more frightening than ever. Tut remained in the darkness, but even his silhouette appeared to be different.

Benjamin instructed us quietly, "The police will be here soon. All we have to do is stall them long enough so our help can get here."

"I think that's what General Custer said to his army just before they were wiped out," Adam quipped.

"Cut it out, Adam. Things look bad enough already," flew out of Becca's mouth. "I say we just run for it and pray they can't catch us." She didn't wait for any of us to answer or agree. Becca took off at full speed.

Benjamin and Adam ran directly toward Tut's aide and quickly split as they neared him. I was behind them but couldn't decide which direction to head. *Father, I'm in trouble again. But whatever happens, I know that you're with me.*

My indecision cost me. Tut cut me off. He snatched me by my sweatshirt, jerking me off my feet. I went flying along the floor. I looked up to see both mummies in the bright light.

124

Bright light! Where did the bright light come from? Was this the bright light that nearly dead people say you see? I tried to scoot away on my hands and the cotton bottom of my shorts, but the two mummies kept getting closer.

"Don't take another step, boys. This is the police," a deep voice called from the room's entrance. The mummies froze and raised their hands in the air.

I jumped to my feet and blinked my eyes to get used to the brightness. The police moved in closer to the mummies.

"Adam, Becca, Benjamin, all the clues said these two weren't real mummies. But because we expected them to be real, we were sure they were. I think it's time to solve the mystery of the curse of King Tut," I told them as I eyed our two opponents.

I unwrapped the face of the boy king, Tut. My suspicions were correct. It wasn't Tut. It was just a man wrapped in linen. "Remember the jewel we found? I began to suspect that these two weren't real mummies, but the jewel thieves that I read about in the newspaper. Clues like their taking our walkie-talkies and flashlights and his linen not smelling like a real mummy's made me think we weren't facing prune people," I told the others.

One of the police officers pulled Tut's hands down out of the air and put handcuffs on him. He did the same to Tut's aide.

The officer next to me spoke, "Well, if it isn't Nails Bopp, the famous jewel thief. I bet that your buddy over there in the Halloween suit is Bobby Jones." The officer motioned with his gun to his partner, "Why don't you help Mr. Jones out of his Christmas wrappings. Although, I do like my criminals gift wrapped."

The guy we'd called Tut said, "Listen, Officer Stoner, I'll be glad to go to jail. Just get me away from these kids. It's less dangerous in prison than it is trying to chase this group away."

The officer smirked and asked, "So, what was your plan this time, Nails?"

"It would have been simple if it weren't for these kids. We dressed as mummies and hid in a display until the museum was closed. We were going to grab what we wanted and slip out when the museum opened tomorrow. But we kept running into these four. We tried to scare them away while we snatched up the gold and jewels. But these little creeps kept coming up with plans to catch us. No one told us that kids would be camping out in here. Isn't that illegal or something?" Nails asked.

The museum curator stepped forward, and my dad was at his side. The curator said, "As far as I'm concerned, these kids can live here at the museum. They saved our valuable collections of antiquities. I don't know how we'll be able to thank them."

"Let's go, boys. I think it's time for you two to get back behind prison bars. Maybe the judge will keep you there this time," the officer said. The two men in blue grabbed the burglars and escorted them out of the room.

Dad came up to me and asked, "Are you all right?"

"I'm fine, Dad, but I've decided that I don't want to be an Egyptologist. You guys lead too dangerous a life for me, and that's only in a museum."

Dad laughed and gave me a big hug. "I want to hear every detail of what happened."

The curator added, "I want to hear the story as well."

Officer Stoner added from the doorway, "I'd appreciate it if you four kids would come down to the station tomorrow and give us a statement."

"Maybe I should put it on video and sell copies of it. I could get an eight hundred number and everything. Call 1 - 8 0 0 - M U M M I E S," I joked.

"We'll talk about that tomorrow," my father said as he put his arm around me.

We walked back to the pyramid and settled on our sleeping bags. I turned to the others and said, "I think we need to pray and thank God for protecting us tonight."

They all nodded their heads in agreement, and Dad motioned for me to pray. "Heavenly Father, you answered our prayers. You protected us like you did David when he prayed in the Psalms for your help. I want to thank you not only for protecting us, but also for demonstrating that we can trust you, even in the toughest situations. In Jesus' name, Amen."

Then we told Dad and the curator the whole story. We may have left out a few little things, like how scared we were, but none of us thought those parts were important. The thing that was most important to me was how God had protected us through the whole mysterious adventure.

We smiled at each other, turned off our flashlights, and lay down. Dad stayed with us the rest of the night. He had finished most of his work on the hieroglyphics. We all felt safer and slept well after our night of racing around the Shield Museum.

The next morning, as we packed up our sleeping bags, knapsacks, and other junk, Adam seemed very quiet.

"What's wrong, Adam?" Benjamin asked his friend.

"If those guys were only burglars, then I still have to face the real curse of King Tut. Remember, I'm the one who touched his stuff," he said with a little shiver.

Dad overheard and made us all sit down. He told Adam, "The curse of King Tut does not exist. It was made up."

"Then why did all those crazy things happen?"

"Some of them have ordinary explanations—like two guys dressed up as mummies pushed you in a dry pond. Other things were just coincidences," Dad answered.

"But what about all those guys who got killed or died mysteriously?" Adam pressed.

"I shouldn't have tried to spook you when we talked about the curse. Let me tell you the rest of the story. When Carnarvon and Carter found the pyramid, they gave an exclusive story to one of the newspapers. Not to be outdone, a rival newspaper made up the curse of Tut," Dad told us.

"What about all the deaths? How do you explain all the people who died?" Adam challenged.

"In some cases, the men were already sick. In others, the people were elderly and the strenuous work pushed their bodies to the limit. They gave out and people died," he reported.

"The museum worker wasn't old. He wasn't sick. Why did he die?" Adam shot another tough question at my father.

"The museum where that was supposed to have happened never had a piece of Tutankhamen's treasure in their collection. If a worker died, it wasn't because of the curse," Dad responded. I was glad that he was taking the time to explain to Adam what had happened.

On the way out to the car we teased each other and joked around. After we had loaded up the trunk, my dad turned to us and said, "Oh, I forgot to tell you. Since I didn't get all of my work with the translations done, the museum invited me to spend a night next weekend to finish up. Anyone up for another sleep-out in the pyramid?"

I rolled my eyes. In unison we screamed, "No!" Then the five of us broke out laughing.

Read and collect all of
Fred E. Katz's

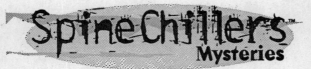

*Turn the page
for a spine-chilling preview . . .*

Stay Tuned for Terror

Book #10
by Fred E. Katz

"Run for it!" Matthew yelled. I was the first one out of the kitchen, but I did not know which way to go. I headed down the hallway where the photos were.

The hall ended at the living room, and just beyond that was the foyer. There was a light on in the living room that gave the foyer a dim, gray look. It was an improvement over a dark black room.

I could see that the front door to the house was no longer barred. As I ran, I prayed, *Thank you, Father, for giving us a way out. At least I think it is. If it isn't, then I need to trust that you'll protect us.*

"Keep running," I yelled. "The front door is no longer blocked." We hit the foyer's slippery marble floor and skidded to a stop in front of the door. My hand shot out toward the knob. Before I could grab it, Kari knocked my hand away and pointed to a note nailed to the door.

Matthew ripped the note off and opened it. It read, "If you want to pass the screen test, go to the recreation room on the other side of the living room."

Juan cheered. "See, it wasn't that bad. Let's get to the rec room and sign the contract to become the next hosts of *Tales of Terror*. This is going to be great."

Matthew slowed him down and pointed out, "Juan, it doesn't say that we've passed the test. It only says to go to the rec room if we want to pass the test."

"That's the same thing," Juan argued.

"No, it isn't," I added to the argument.

"I guess the only way to find out is to go to the rec room and see what's there," Juan challenged.

We were a little more cautious as we walked back through the living room and into another hallway. It was longer and I felt like we were heading to the back of the haunted mansion. The hallway got darker as we went farther. It came to an abrupt stop in front of a large set of double doors.

"I guess this is when we find out if we're the hosts, or if we still have more screen test to go," Matthew said.

"Let's go in and see who is right," Juan suggested.

He opened the door. It was dimly lit, but what a room it was. It had a Ping-Pong table, a pool table, three pinball machines, and a large-screen TV with popcorn and soda sitting in front of it.

"This is fantastic," Matthew said. "I have to admit that Juan was right. We must have passed the test. I guess we're supposed to chill here until someone comes to meet us."

Kari and I jumped over the back of the big, over-stuffed couch in front of the TV. I snapped open a can of soda and took a small swig. I didn't even trust America's favorite cola in this place. It tasted good, so I downed the rest of it in a couple of gulps. I had not realized how thirsty I could get when I'm being scared to death.

"This is some set-up. It must be where we hang out whenever we're not on the air. I could get to like this," Kari said to me. We both laughed, and I leaned back on the couch, picking up the remote control. I pushed the button and the TV came on.

It was a fitting show. It was about kids being chased through a haunted house. Pretty typical stuff and not very scary after you have actually experienced it.

Matthew and Juan sat next to us on the couch. Juan leaned forward, grabbed a soda, and said, "I'm trying to think about what I'm going to say to all the kids at school."

"Tell them the truth. We are the most awesome set of hosts that *Tales of Terror* will ever have," Kari responded.

"I guess that will do," he said, and then laughed.

Matthew sucked in a breath and let it out slowly. "I was just thinking."

"Wow, you thought twice in one night. This ought to be in the *Guinness Book of World Records*," Juan joked. I could tell he was relaxing. Juan and Matthew always joked around when they were just hanging out.

"Real funny!" Matthew tossed back. "I was wondering, what if the monsters and all the other stuff had been real instead of fake? What would we do?"

"We could draw on the spiritual warfare stuff in the Bible. Pastor Smith mentioned it last Sunday in his message," Kari said thoughtfully.

"I think you're onto something here," I told her.

Kari continued, "In the Book of Ephesians it tells us that we don't wrestle against real people when it comes to spiritual things. We wrestle against unseen beings from the devil's army."

"I remember that section. My question is, what are we supposed to do?" Matthew asked.

"Pastor Smith said that we need to put on spiritual armor," Kari answered.

I was confused. "How do we get spiritual armor? I must have missed that part."

"He plans to talk about that part next Sunday," Kari answered.

"Then I'm there even if I have to walk," Matthew told us.

"I'm coming with you," Juan added. He settled onto the couch. "Does anyone know what's going on in this movie?"

"The last I noticed, four kids were being chased through a haunted house. When we started talking, I lost track of the plot," I replied.

"It must be an upcoming episode of *Tales of Terror* because the four kids are sitting in this room. Look, behind them is a monster. That is such an old trick. Why couldn't they come up with something a little more original than a monster sneaking up on unsuspecting kids? That never really happens," Juan griped.

"Actually the plot isn't from a new episode. It looks a lot like the movie *Don't Open the Door.* But that movie was in black and white. This must be a remake of it," Matthew told us.

"I'll bet it's going to be the first episode we host. We should watch it—think of it as homework," Juan said with a laugh.

We sat watching the four kids on the TV. The camera angle made it difficult to see what they looked like. One thing was very strange. The kids in the movie were dressed exactly like we were. The monster on the TV kept inching its way closer to the characters. They sat with their backs to the slimy creature. They didn't even know it was sneaking up behind them.

"This is stupid. Monsters just don't sneak up on people," Matthew said, and he leaned forward to get another soda. I noticed that one of the kids on TV leaned forward at the same time. So I tried it. I leaned forward. The kid on the TV did too.

"I've got some very disturbing news. Those four kids are us. There must be a camera on us," I told them. I tried not to show my panic.

"That's crazy," Kari said. "If that was us on TV, there would be a monster behind us." We all turned around together. There behind us, inches from taking a bite out of Kari's head, was the monster from the TV.

"Ahhhhhh!" we screamed in unison.